THISTLEWOOD MANOR:

MURDER AT THE HEDGEROW

(An Eliza Montagu Cozy Mystery—Book One)

FIONA GRACE

Fiona Grace

Fiona Grace is author of the LACEY DOYLE COZY MYSTERY series, comprising nine books; of the TUSCAN VINEYARD COZY MYSTERY series, comprising seven books; of the DUBIOUS WITCH COZY MYSTERY series, comprising three books; of the BEACHFRONT BAKERY COZY MYSTERY series, comprising six books; of the CATS AND DOGS COZY MYSTERY series, comprising nine books; and of the ELIZA MONTAGU COZY MYSTERY series, comprising three books (and counting).

Fiona would love to hear from you, so please visit www.fionagraceauthor.com to receive free ebooks, hear the latest news, and stay in touch.

BOOKS BY FIONA GRACE

ELIZA MONTAGU COZY MYSTERY
MURDER AT THE HEDGEROW (Book #1)
A DALLOP OF DEATH (Book #2)
CALAMITY AT THE BALL (Book #3)

LACEY DOYLE COZY MYSTERY
MURDER IN THE MANOR (Book#1)
DEATH AND A DOG (Book #2)
CRIME IN THE CAFE (Book #3)
VEXED ON A VISIT (Book #4)
KILLED WITH A KISS (Book #5)
PERISHED BY A PAINTING (Book #6)
SILENCED BY A SPELL (Book #7)
FRAMED BY A FORGERY (Book #8)
CATASTROPHE IN A CLOISTER (Book #9)

TUSCAN VINEYARD COZY MYSTERY
AGED FOR MURDER (Book #1)
AGED FOR DEATH (Book #2)
AGED FOR MAYHEM (Book #3)
AGED FOR SEDUCTION (Book #4)
AGED FOR VENGEANCE (Book #5)
AGED FOR ACRIMONY (Book #6)
AGED FOR MALICE (Book #7)

DUBIOUS WITCH COZY MYSTERY
SKEPTIC IN SALEM: AN EPISODE OF MURDER (Book #1)
SKEPTIC IN SALEM: AN EPISODE OF CRIME (Book #2)
SKEPTIC IN SALEM: AN EPISODE OF DEATH (Book #3)

BEACHFRONT BAKERY COZY MYSTERY
BEACHFRONT BAKERY: A KILLER CUPCAKE (Book #1)
BEACHFRONT BAKERY: A MURDEROUS MACARON (Book #2)
BEACHFRONT BAKERY: A PERILOUS CAKE POP (Book #3)

BEACHFRONT BAKERY: A DEADLY DANISH (Book #4)
BEACHFRONT BAKERY: A TREACHEROUS TART (Book #5)
BEACHFRONT BAKERY: A CALAMITOUS COOKIE (Book #6)

CATS AND DOGS COZY MYSTERY
A VILLA IN SICILY: OLIVE OIL AND MURDER (Book #1)
A VILLA IN SICILY: FIGS AND A CADAVER (Book #2)
A VILLA IN SICILY: VINO AND DEATH (Book #3)
A VILLA IN SICILY: CAPERS AND CALAMITY (Book #4)
A VILLA IN SICILY: ORANGE GROVES AND VENGEANCE
(Book #5)
A VILLA IN SICILY: CANNOLI AND A CASUALTY (Book #6)
A VILLA IN SICILY: SPAGHETTI AND SUSPICION (Book #7)
A VILLA IN SICILY: LEMONS AND A PREDICAMENT (Book #8)
A VILLA IN SICILY: GELATO AND A VENDETTA (Book #9)

CHAPTER ONE

Eliza smiled defiantly at the men yelling at her, their fists clenched and their faces red with anger. In the beginning, it scared her, but it was almost like a game to her now. Sometimes she would watch them for fun, waiting for them to pop like a balloon.

The men hurled insults at Eliza and her fellow suffragettes as they marched along Oxford Street. While many of the other women tried to blend in, Eliza stood out from the crowd—her crimson coat and beret a red rag to the bulls screaming from the sidelines.

Eliza's friend Patty was less bold. She walked sheepishly beside Eliza, her dark green overcoat and glasses allowing her to blend seamlessly into the crowd.

"They're so...angry," Patty said. Eliza could tell she was intimidated, but she clutched the large, white "Votes for Women" sign in her hands and raised it a little higher anyway.

Eliza smiled at her friend. "Some of them are every bit as angry as they look, but most of them are just going along with the mob. That's why we march—to persuade the ones who don't really mean it."

"What about the ones who do mean it?"

"Oh, them? We'll toss them into the Thames. I always find that cold water is the quickest way to sober the mind."

Eliza laughed. It was May of 1928, and the rumors that the British government was getting ready to concede and give all women the right to vote abounded. Hope was in the air. She could feel it in her bones.

I have to capture this moment, Eliza thought, as she looked around at her fellow suffragettes and the angry mob following them. She closed her eyes for a moment, committing these sights to memory.

As soon as I get home, she thought, *I'm going to paint this.*

"Where's yer fellas, ladies? At home wearin' an apron?" a voice shouted in Patty's direction, echoing up and above the crowds of taunting men and bouncing between the elegant facades of London's most glamorous street. Several of the men nearby laughed in response.

Eliza studied Patty to make sure that she was okay. All of the women were singing the chorus of "March of the Women" now, and she watched as Patty punctuated each note a little more strongly and held her sign a little higher. She could tell she was trying to project

1

confidence—to make it clear that she would not be intimidated, but Eliza knew her friend. She could tell Patty was rattled.

Eliza toyed with the idea of engaging with the heckler. At a previous protest, she had soaked a crowd of red-faced misogynists with a fire extinguisher. The police searched the crowd for her after that, but she ditched her characteristic red beret and blended into anonymity with her fellow protesters.

Taking this man down a peg would feel good, no doubt, but she wasn't sure how Patty would feel about it. Patty had never been nearly as comfortable with conflict as Eliza was.

Eliza had almost decided to let it go when the man taunted the women again.

"What you all need is a good seein' to. Form a queue, ladies. I'll help ya out."

Again, laughter came in response from the men, and Patty blushed nervously at the man's words. Eliza could tell from the way Patty's protest sign trembled that her hands were shaking.

Eliza could not let that stand.

She moved through the protesters, pulling Patty along beside her, until she was right next to the heckler.

"Oi! Ladies!" the man said with a grin. "How about..."

"How about what, darling?" Eliza said loudly, adjusting her red beret as she stopped in front of the man and stared him down.

At first, he seemed apprehensive, but then he let out a bellowing laugh and looked around to the other men on the street. "Fellas! Looks like we've got a couple of goers here."

"Darling...Whatever do you mean?" Eliza asked, her voice sweet and her innocence feigned.

"I think you know what I mean, Lovely."

"Little old me?" Eliza asked as she moved closer to him. "I'm terribly sorry, but I can't say that I do. Could you explain it to me? I have no idea what a 'goer' is, but I'd really like to know."

"Well...I..." the man stammered.

"Please tell me and my lady friends. You seem to know a lot about it."

Eliza stepped closer and turned on the charm. She could almost hear the collective sigh of her family back home as she did. She knew they would be mortified by her behavior, but she'd certainly never let that stop her before, and she wasn't about to start now.

Reaching out her hand, Eliza ran her finger up the man's arm. "What was it you called us? 'A couple of goers'? What did you mean, exactly?"

"Now...listen h...here!" The man stammered.

"If you are a goer..." Eliza leaned in, "Perhaps you should have a go of this!"

With that, Eliza swiftly pulled the protest sign out of Patty's hands and slipped the wood it was mounted on down the back of the man's jacket. Before he even had a moment to process what had happened, Eliza had wrapped her arm around his shoulders and pulled him into the crowd.

"Sisters! We've got a new supporter!" she yelled.

Cheers went up in the crowd as the red-faced man was welcomed with a sea of hands. He was so caught off guard and outnumbered that he had little choice but to be pulled into the crowd by the suffragettes, swept along with them, all the while looking for help that was not forthcoming.

Eliza turned her attention back to the other men on the pavement and smiled. "Who else wants to join the cause?"

Several of the men looked down at their watches, as if late for an important meeting, and dispersed in different directions. Patty looked at Eliza and smiled.

"Hope you don't mind me borrowing your sign," Eliza said.

"Not at all," Patty said. "I can't imagine a better use for it."

Both Eliza and Patty watched the heckler for a moment, giggling at the sight of him swallowed up by the crowd, the "Votes for Women" sign proudly protruding from his jacket.

This is the moment I want to immortalize on canvas, Eliza thought. She couldn't wait to get home and recreate the scene as exactly as possible, though she knew she would have to make one notable alteration. When it came time to memorialize the moment, she would have to remove herself from the image. No matter how much she might want to, she knew she couldn't include herself in the painting. Her past forbade that.

***

Two hours later, as the evening sun began to dip in the sky over downtown London, Eliza returned to her flat on Carol Terrace. The building was ornate, with white marble pillars flanking the main door and a picturesque central staircase inside leading up to her third-floor apartment. Eliza both adored that place and resented it. She loved the privacy and independence it afforded her, and the location was ideal, but it never really felt like her. It was still filled with antique furniture from a bygone era, and it didn't even have a telephone line installed. But it was what the flat represented that stayed with her like a stone in her shoe: she wasn't really independent at all. This flat, like everything else in her life, was paid for entirely with her father's money.

Eliza unlocked the door and headed into the study, where she wound up her gramophone player and put on her favorite Papa Jack record. Eliza loved jazz, almost as much as she loved painting, and she was convinced that if she ever found the time, she would learn to play such music herself one day. Tonight, however, the easel and canvas awaited her.

Eliza took off her red beret and began taking her blond locks out of the pins that held them until her soft curls relaxed to just above her shoulders. She slipped on her paint-flecked smock and grabbed a fresh canvas. Using a pencil first, Eliza began to sketch the scene she had been part of just a few hours before. Protesters walked the streets, valiantly marching for the right to vote, while the heckler and his friends jeered from the pavement.

She stood back for a moment and studied the sketch. There were a few things she would change before she added the paint, but all in all, she was quite pleased with it. The technique was good, but more importantly, she felt confident that she'd captured the spirit of the thing.

Too bad no one will ever see it, she thought.

In her soul, Eliza knew she was a painter. The only problem was that she hadn't actually managed to convince the rest of the world of that fact yet. In her paintings, Eliza explored the experience of speaking truth to power and mocked the antiquated way British society was constructed. If she had been a girl from a working-class home, this might have been deemed revolutionary and resonant. But as an upper-class girl who grew up on a fancy family estate, her paintings just came off as "a cry for attention from a bored little rich girl"—or, at least, that's what her mother and Great Aunt Martha always used to say.

Eliza was jolted from her thoughts by a knock on the door.

How odd, she thought. After all, it was fairly late in the evening now, and she wasn't expecting anyone.

She opened the door to find a kid, about fifteen years old, if that, holding a letter. Eliza signed for it, gave him a tip, and then closed the door.

Her heart raced as she stared at the envelope in her hands. She recognized the handwriting on the front of the envelope immediately. It was her mother—her mother with whom she had not spoken in three years.

Growing up, Eliza had adored her mother. She wanted nothing more than her attention and approval. But as she grew older, it became increasingly clear that Eliza was going to have to choose between having her mother's affection and being true to who she was. Eliza was not one to sit down and be quiet. She was someone who wanted to stand up and be counted. And her mother would simply never understand or allow that.

It was an agonizing choice—one that ultimately forced her from the only life and home she'd ever known—but in spite of it all, she had never regretted it. Not even for a moment. The cost of staying was simply too high. Eliza wanted adventure. She wanted to break the mold and fight for things that mattered. Much as she wished it wasn't the case, she was never going to be able to do that at Thistlewood House.

When Eliza left, her mother swore that she would never speak to her again. She said that by leaving, Eliza was abandoning the family and rejecting everything they stood for. Her mother swore this was a decision she could not walk back from, and Eliza believed her. Her mother was nothing if not true to her word and firm in her convictions.

And yet, here was this letter.

Eliza's hands shook as she took her ivory-handled letter opener from the mantel in the drawing room and prepared to open the envelope. She wasn't sure what news the letter contained, but she knew one thing for certain: If her mother was reaching out to her after all of this time, it could not be good.

CHAPTER TWO

"You can make it," she whispered to herself as she weaved through a sea of besuited men in fedora hats reading broadsheet papers and creating as much smoke from their cigarettes as the nearby steam trains.

Eliza knew that lateness would mean disaster. Her mother was a stickler for punctuality and urgency. If Eliza didn't make it to Thistlewood House by the afternoon, there would be hell to pay.

As she approached the large, blue steam engine on platform 4 with six red carriages behind it, Eliza saw the platform attendant looking at his watch. The driver of the engine, his hands and face smeared in black soot, was leaning out of a window seemingly waiting for the whistle to get under way—which it did just moments before Eliza arrived at the platform.

"Wait!" Eliza yelled as the blue steam engine's wheels slowly began to move. "Wait!"

Running past the conductor, she thrust one of her suitcases into his arms.

"I need your help," she said.

In the confusion, he obeyed, and followed her as fast as he could.

The train was now slowly moving, but Eliza managed to grab hold of the nearest red carriage door. It would not budge, and as she tried her best to keep up with the train along the platform, the attendant behind her huffed and puffed, running with her largest suitcase in his arms under his chin.

Eliza was starting to sweat now. The idea of being late filled her with dread. Thankfully, it also filled her with an unexpected surge of strength, so this time, when she tugged on the carriage door again, it suddenly swung open. Standing in the doorway was a tall man in a perfectly pressed grey suit, his blond hair slicked back neatly. "Need a hand?" he asked.

"Catch!" Eliza said, as she hurled her smallest suitcase at him.

He caught it, so she tossed him the next one, which he caught as well. Finally, as the train gathered speed, she grabbed hold of his hand and jumped into the carriage, followed by the huffing and puffing platform attendant. As the train accelerated, the steam from its engine flowing over the sides of the carriage outside, Eliza's momentum pushed her forward, knocking the man who had helped to the ground and tossing Eliza on top of him.

Eliza didn't blush often, but as she pulled herself off of the handsome stranger she'd inadvertently toppled on to, she could feel her cheeks go scarlet.

"That's certainly one way to make an entrance," the man said with a smile, as he rose to his feet and offered Eliza his hand.

"I considered using the stairs, but this way seemed far more exciting" she said, straightening her dress and grinning back at him.

The attendant, meanwhile, stood behind her, staring out the window, muttering quietly to himself: "I'm not even supposed to be on this train."

Eliza offered to write a letter of apology and thanks to his boss before taking her seat by the window and immediately getting lost in the countryside. Her artist's mind was so ablaze with the striking images outside her window that she did not even bother to peruse the Art Nouveau prints in the copy of *Pan Magazine* she had brought with her. The world was just too alive to ignore, even for a good read.

Eliza watched as the city relinquished its grip to the English countryside. Rolling hills, deep woods, and winding rivers were lush with the green of summer. This rich show of nature was in stark contrast to the buildings and bustling streets of London that had preceded it; though both were, to Eliza, mesmerizing in their own, beautiful way.

As the train pulled into the station, Eliza immediately felt the pull of home. She had missed the place so much, and the idea of finally seeing her father and her siblings after all this time filled her with joy. But she also felt something else: fear. It had been years since Eliza had last set foot in Thistlewood House, and she had left with good reason. She wasn't sure she was ready to be back—to feel the sting of rejection again.

"Good day, Miss," a voice said, pulling Eliza out of her thoughts. She recognized the man immediately. It was Statue Stevenson—as he was known on her family estate—her father's driver.

"Good Day, Stevenson," Eliza said.

Seeing Stevenson, she felt a tug of nostalgia. She had always had a soft spot for him, and this marked the first time she had seen anyone from her home in quite some time.

"I gather your train journey was uneventful?" Stevenson said, standing there in his black driver's suit and hat. He remained stiff as a post, hence his nickname, and there was not the slightest flicker of emotion on his face.

"Yes...It's good to see you, Stevenson, Old Bean. How is your daughter?"

"Adequate. Sally is now a Governess over at Barnsley Hall. We are pleased, I suppose. If you like that sort of thing."

"And what have you been doing these last few years, Stevenson? Anything new and exciting?" Eliza asked, despite already knowing the answer. It was Stevenson, after all.

"New? Why would there be anything new, Miss? I am not a believer in new things."

"As riveting as ever, Stevenson," she said, patting him on the arm and winking at him so he would know that she was being playful. "This drive will just fly in."

Stevenson led Eliza to her father's horse and carriage. The horses were white thoroughbreds, and the carriage was dark blue with gold leaf decorations. No expense was spared.

For a moment, Eliza wished he had sent the limousine. It would certainly have been faster. But what the carriage lacked in speed, it made up for in panache and nostalgia. The moment she stepped inside, Eliza was immediately taken back to childhood drives around the country with her father. It was a comforting memory—and with her mother's ominous summons looming large in her mind, comfort was exactly what she needed.

"Say, Stevenson, you wouldn't happen to know anything about why mother has called me back here, would you?"

"I do not, Miss. I make it a point not to know things."

Eliza sighed and stared out the window as the horses began clip-clopping along country roads. She'd figured as much, but still, she wished Stevenson had some information to offer. The idea of returning home might not have seemed so frightening if she at least understood why she was being summoned.

As the landscape unfolded before her, emerald hills stretched as far as the eye could see, and the tall green grass and cornfields that populated them swayed in the afternoon breeze. It was a sight Eliza knew intimately—one she did not realize how much she had missed until this moment. She would have sketched them if her sketchbook had been at hand.

Instead, she tried to break the urge to create with some conversation. "Any good jokes, Stevenson?" she asked loudly.

"No, Miss. I'm not a fan of jokes."

"Thanks, Stevenson...Never mind, I'm sure there'll be plenty to laugh about when we get home."

"Quite, Miss."

Eliza began to recognize the countryside around her, and with each passing mile, the world felt more and more like home. In time, the rolling green hills around her parted, and beyond, a large section of forest came to dominate the scene. And then, there they were...The gates to Thistlewood House itself, high and monumental.

The path into the Thistlewood estate moved through the woodland, bending and twisting. There was something magical about it. Suddenly, Eliza realized that her heart was racing. Much to her surprise, beneath the dread of having to face her family, there was something else too. Excitement. Every inch of that path and wood held a story for her. The weeping willow tree where she had her first kiss with Harry, the butler's son; the bubbling brook she fell into while trying to convince her friends that the rope swing she had built was perfectly safe; the apple orchard where she had gone to cry in private when she heard that her favorite uncle had died.

These memories overwhelmed Eliza, and in that moment, she felt almost happy to be coming home. There was a mystery to the grounds, filled with promise and intrigue, and Eliza found herself eager to once again explore them. But, she reminded herself as soon as she noticed the unexpected optimism, there was also mystery and intrigue in her mother's letter—and whatever that mystery was, Eliza was fairly certain she was going to be anything but happy about it.

The trees parted and the tall red sandstone of Thistlewood House came into view, surrounded by sprawling green lawns and the garden maze to the East. Stevenson finally brought the carriage to a stop at the foot of the steep, marble stairs, and Eliza, eager to stretch her legs, stepped out immediately.

Moments later, Eliza heard the sound of feet running down the marble stairs. Long, blond hair bounced and flowed on the shoulders of a figure Eliza knew only too well. Two arms wrapped themselves instantly around Eliza and the giggling began.

"I can't believe you're here!" Eliza's sister, Mercy, said with glee.

Eliza had always been close to Mercy, much to her mother's chagrin. Mercy was less rebellious than her sister. Like Eliza, she had been taught from a very young age that the future of upper-class

England, and indeed of the Empire, was to marry up—or, at the very least—equal. It was a pureblood approach to the Class System that their parents held dear, but Eliza despised. As such, in her mother's view, Mercy was their only hope for a respectable daughter.

Mercy had therefore been rigorously raised, coached, and educated to be the perfect bride for another member of High Society. But Eliza had secretly planted the seed of revolt within her, often over late-night talks in the kitchen with mugs of hot chocolate and the writings of Charlotte Perkins Gilman. Mercy was still far more compliant than Eliza, but Eliza knew she had secretly sparked a more modern outlook in her sister.

"I saw the carriage on the path, so I had to come out first." Mercy said. She smiled at Eliza, her bright, blue eyes and beauty spot on her cheek were almost as dazzling as the white, cotton dress she was wearing. "I'm so glad you're here."

"I had no choice," Eliza said. "Not after mother's letter…How is Father?"

Mercy leaned in and did her best to obscure her words from any would-be eavesdroppers. "The thing is, I think they've asked you here because—"

Before she could finish, Eliza's older brothers both came bounding down the stairs.

"Eliza!" Melville said, a grin spreading across his face.

"Hello, Sister," Cedric added, his words escaping along with a puff of pipe smoke. "It is agreeable to see you." He stood stoically, his black hair slicked back, and his tweed suit complete with a red velvet tie—a stark against the deep sandstone of Thistlewood House.

Cedric broke character for a moment, winking at his little sister, before taking her hand and affectionately squeezing it. "I hope things haven't been too rough," he whispered in her ear.

Cedric was a true product of upper-class conditioning, putting him at odds with Eliza's beliefs, yet Eliza loved him deeply. Melville was a bit more like her—caught between the old and new ways. He was happy to reap the rewards of modernity, especially when it came to his love life, but unlike Eliza, he was also happy to lead a life of luxury, comfortable in the conceit of his privilege.

"How have you and Melville been without me here to keep you both in line?"

"I have been excellent," Cedric replied. "Melville on the other hand…"

"Well, one of us has to keep mother on her toes, and with you gone, dear sister, the task naturally fell to me. It is a large responsibility, but I think I've borne it admirably."

Melville laughed as he stepped forward and wrapped his arms around his sister.

"It's so good to see you, Sis!" he said.

His brown hair had receded quite a bit since Eliza had last seen him, but he wore the same boyish grin on his face that he always had, and Eliza was filled with a rush of affection at the sight of it.

"It's good to see you too. I've missed you. In fact," she turned to address her family, "I've missed you all."

"You've yet to see Great Aunt Martha," Melville said.

Eliza laughed, but before she could say anything else, the shrill voice of Great Aunt Martha fluttered through as though she had been summoned: "Nephew! Is she here!?"

Eliza felt her blood run cold. Just hearing that voice again—that same accusatory tone that had finally convinced her to leave home three years ago—was enough to send her heart into her stomach.

But then, she heard another voice—that of her father, Lord Montagu, whose head was sticking out of a recently opened window.

"Eliza, my girl," he boomed. "I'm so glad you made it. I was worried that Stevenson might have gotten lost again."

Turning, Eliza lurched back, startled. Stevenson had been standing behind her the entire time. "My God, Stevenson. You really don't make any noise, do you?"

"I don't believe in noise, Miss. Never cared for that sort of thing."

"My dear," Lord Montagu continued from above. "I hate to do this, but it is imperative that I see you at once in my study."

Eliza opened her mouth to reply, but before she could, he had already shut the window.

Eliza took a deep breath and tried to steady her nerves before making the ascent into Thistlewood House. She was unsure exactly what awaited her there—what news her father might be about to share. But if the look on her siblings' faces was any indication, whatever it was, it definitely was not good.

CHAPTER THREE

Entering Thistlewood House made Eliza feel whole again. It was as though she had left a fragment of her soul behind there, somewhere hidden in a room or secret passageway, and she imagined that there was an echo of her childhood self here now, dreaming of adventure and the open horizon.

She knew that little girl would be proud of the woman she had become and would love to be regaled with tales of the adventures that she had had. But she also knew that they had come at a cost. Leaving her family and her home, Eliza had lost a piece of herself—a piece she did not realize was so important until she came back here again.

It's been too long, she thought.

Eliza watched the servants swirl around her. They moved around at pace and with purpose, which Eliza knew from experience meant they were preparing for the arrival of someone important. Eliza had never been comfortable with this sort of social hierarchy—the idea that the mere presence of wealth or a title meant someone was important. She wanted to stop the servants, to tell them that whoever it was that was coming was not worth the fuss, but she knew better. If there was anything growing up in this house had taught her, it was that this estate, and the people in it, were not yet ready for such new and radical ideas.

Truth be told, she wasn't sure they were ready for her either.

The main staircase was as splendid as ever. Its rich mahogany wood spiraled up several levels to the glorious mosaic roof and twin chandeliers shining far above. As Eliza climbed upwards, she once again found herself staring at the oil paintings that hung on the walls. There was at least a dozen of them—all portraits—and while Eliza typically loved paintings of all types, she had never liked these. She always felt their watchful eyes were accusatory, following visitors around the room as if they should not be there. Telling her that, even though she was a Montagu, she did not belong.

As she reached the next level on her way to her father's study, Eliza looked up and saw another set of eyes staring at her, only this time, they were not painted in oil. An unfamiliar man with an intense gaze and a bald head was on the top level, peering over the banister directly at Eliza.

Before she could even so much as call out "Hello," the man pulled back and disappeared. There was something menacing about the way he had looked at her that unnerved Eliza, and she wanted to try and follow him—to learn more about this mysterious man—but she could not waste any more time. Not when she still didn't know why she had been summoned home or if her father was alright.

***

The door to his study was closed. The dark oak was like an entitled barrier to the world, one Eliza knew her father often used to protect himself from the stresses of life. She wondered what sort of stresses he might be hiding from now. She worried that she might not be ready to find out the answer.

Her hand shook slightly as she knocked on the thick, wooden door. Her father's voice was muffled but unmistakable.

"Come in!"

Whatever the news, you can handle it, Eliza thought, trying to reassure herself as she turned the brass doorknob and anxiously entered her father's study.

The room was relatively small compared to many of the others at Thistlewood House. The combination of the large fireplace and the wall of rich, leather-bound books gave the room a sense of coziness. Much like the antique globe map on her father's desk and the framed Indian folk art next to the door, the books were largely just for show. She was quite sure neither her father nor anyone else in the family had ever actually read them.

"Eliza!" Lord Montagu exclaimed, as he moved from around his desk and came to embrace her. He held her in his arms for a moment before pulling back to study her.

"You're looking well, I trust your journey was uneventful?"

Eliza didn't even bother to answer the question. She knew that would have deeply bothered her mother—after all, it was a violation of etiquette to ignore a question and abruptly change the subject, and her mother abhorred etiquette violations—but Eliza didn't care. She had to know what was going on.

"Father, please, tell me what's going on." Eliza said, pulling out her mother's letter from her inside coat pocket. "Mother said I had to come urgently. That you needed me. Is everything alright? Are you ill?"

Lord Montagu's expression softened, his shoulders slouching slightly from their usual regimental stance. "Oh, Liza, my girl. Yes, I'm alright. But you...Whatever am I going to do with you?"

"Me?" Suddenly, the feeling of fear Eliza had felt was replaced by a very specific sense of dread—a sense of dread she had not felt since she left Thistlewood House three years prior.

Something was afoot.

"Yes, you, Darling..." Lord Montagu said, as he moved towards a small cabinet of polished wood, which he opened, taking out a bottle of whiskey and pouring two large glasses.

Eliza couldn't help smiling in spite of herself as her father walked one of the glasses over to her. Typically, whiskey was reserved for the men of the house, but Eliza had always preferred it to the more "lady-like" drinks her mother insisted she select. Her father sharing the whiskey with her was a small act of rebellion—one Eliza had always appreciated. She knew it was his brief, wordless way of saying he loved her just as she was, and he was in her corner, even if he wasn't always in a position to defend her or her choices.

"Please, will you take a seat?" he said, motioning towards two large armchairs on either side of the fireplace.

Taking the glass and sitting down to the left of the mantelpiece, Eliza stared at the lifeless hearth. There was no need for flames at that time of the day in summer, but the absence of them only added to the sinking feeling in Eliza's stomach.

As Eliza slowly sipped the whiskey, she felt the sting of the peaty spirit, unmistakably an Islay Scotch. It felt good, full of rich, smokey flavor.

"Still nothing but the best, right, father?"

Lord Montagu had not taken a drink just yet. Instead, he held the glass in his right hand as he sat down in the other armchair. Then, he moved the glass around, catching the light from the window. The crystal sparkled.

Eliza kept waiting for him to say something—anything—but instead, he just stared at the drink. Finally, she grew tired of waiting and decided to make conversation in hopes that getting him talking would eventually get him to the point.

"I saw someone strange on my way up here. He was staring down at me from the top floor. Bald headed chap..."

"Ah, yes," Lord Montagu said. "Barnsley. He's an old friend recuperating here for a while. Best to leave him to himself."

"I've never heard you mention—"

"You know I love you, Eliza," Lord Montagu interrupted. "And I have always supported your desire to stay in London and become an artist, but you were born into an important family. That comes with responsibilities to which we must tend."

Eliza's stomach sank to her toes. She knew where this was going, and she would have given anything to stop the conversation before it reached its inevitable conclusion. She wanted nothing more than to have missed that train after all. If she had, she wouldn't be here now, listening to her father try to convince her to disrupt her life and dismantle her dreams.

"Your siblings understand this," Lord Montagu continued. "But you..."

"I'm just...different from the rest of you."

"You say that like it's something to be proud of," Lord Montagu said, turning his gaze to his daughter with a raised, greying eyebrow.

"It's who I am," Eliza said softly. "I love you all. And I respect you very much. But I will not apologize for that."

Lord Montagu lowered his voice as footsteps neared the door to the hallway.

"Just do as your mother says. Please, Eliza. For all our sakes."

And then, as if on cue, a knock sounded.

"Come in, my Darling."

The door opened, and Eliza turned to see her mother standing in the doorway. Eliza was not prepared for just how much her mother had aged in the three years since she'd seen her. Her once brown hair now carried a wisp of grey along the center parting, and her face looked more haggard than the one Eliza had said goodbye to. The last few years had clearly been hard on her, and Eliza couldn't help but wonder just how much she had missed.

Eliza took a deep breath and then stood up. She'd never once even so much as flinched when staring down angry hecklers at a protest, but there was something about her mother's presence in this moment that made Eliza's knees knock.

"It's good to see you," Eliza said, though she wasn't entirely sure that was true.

"And you," Lady Montagu said, stepping forward and kissing her daughter on the cheek.

"Have you told her yet?" Lady Montagu asked, turning to her husband impatiently.

"Well...I—"

"Oh, honestly, Gerald. You're always too soft with her! If only you'd—"

Eliza sat down and listened as her mother and father squabbled. It reminded her of old times. Despite the tension, there was a comfort to it; their barbed words acted like an old, soothing blanket. Eliza sipped her glass and waited for a break in the back and forth that never came.

Eliza finally stood up after finishing her drink. She was tired of waiting.

"Can one of you please just tell me what this is all about?"

"Well—I—You see—The thing is..." Lord Montagu stuttered, clearly unsure how to break the news to his daughter. Eliza knew the fact that he could not even seem to form a sentence definitely was not a good sign.

Lady Montagu rolled her eyes and let out another loud tut. "What your father is trying to say, is that we did call you back here for an emergency, Eliza. The emergency that is your love life."

Eliza felt a flush of red rush to her cheeks. She knew that her mother would interpret that as embarrassment or shame, but it wasn't. It was fury.

"You mean to tell me you scared me half to death and had me travel all this way just to be set up!?"

Eliza paced around the room, fuming, her gaze alternating between both her parents. She expected this sort of thing from her mother, but her father? He had always supported her. Loved her for who she was. And while he had not always agreed with her dreams or her beliefs, he'd respected her right to have them—or, at least, that's what she thought. Looking at him now, she wasn't so sure.

"And who is he? Let me guess, one of Father's business associates, so you can use me to broaden the Montagu empire? Make me part of a negotiation like I'm some sort of chattel?"

"If you would just give him a chance," Lady Montagu insisted, "I'm certain you two would hit it off."

"Hit it off!? The only thing that's 'off' is me. Goodbye!" Eliza said as she stormed towards the door.

"Eliza!" Lady Montagu said in a voice so stern, it stopped Eliza in her tracks.

"Perhaps we should have a nice chat in the garden," her mother continued, her voice suddenly calm and polite in a way that struck Eliza as entirely superficial.

Knowing better than to say no to her mother while she was in this sort of mood, Eliza followed her through the house, down the stairs, and out a pair of French doors.

In front of them was a large, cream-colored marquee tent that covered a section of the rear lawn. Eliza's eyes were drawn to the walled garden off in the distance, a place filled with statues and adventures where she used to play as a child. She wanted to run to that place and relive those carefree days, but instead, Lady Montagu had her locked in, arm-in-arm, as they entered the cool shade of marquee.

Inside, beautiful purple and pink floral decorations had been placed in large, green-gold Georgian vases. Eliza knew that meant business. Those vases were priceless and were only ever brought out for the most important guests.

In the center of the marquee was a large, rectangular dining table, set beautifully with white tablecloths and silver candelabras. Nearby, a blond servant girl in a black maid's uniform was polishing the silver cutlery that was to be placed next to Lady Montagu's prized Chinese Canton Rose dishes.

"Careful with those," Lady Montagu said to the servant briskly as she gestured towards the dishes.

"Of course, Lady Montagu," the girl said anxiously.

Eliza bristled at her mother's way of commanding the servants—never even so much as a please or a thank you—but she remained silent. Her mother, however, did not.

"Eliza, you have left me no choice. All of this has been prepared for you. Please accept it graciously."

Eliza wished her mother thought of the servant as more of a person. If she had, she would never be having this conversation with Eliza. She would never discuss these sorts of things in front of company.

"I am not going to be used as a pawn in the family's business plans."

"You are not a pawn, Eliza. You are our daughter, and as our daughter there are—"

"—certain expectations," Eliza said, joining in with her mother so that the phrase, which Eliza had heard countless times before, was uttered in unison. Her mother glared at her briefly before continuing.

"Lord Darlington is wonderful. A true gentleman from an excellent family. You will attend the dinner this evening and treat him accordingly. And you will stay at Thistlewood until I say otherwise. Do you understand me?"

"What happens if I refuse?"

"Then we're cutting you off. No money. No flat in London. Just you and your paintings, living on the street."

Suddenly, the room around Eliza started swimming. Her breath caught in her throat, and it was as though an elephant had taken up residence on her chest.

"You can't be serious," Eliza said, though she knew full well that wasn't true. Her mother was not the sort of person to make threats unless she fully intended to follow through on them.

"I think we both know I am," her mother replied, her face stern and her tone utterly unsympathetic.

"But if I marry him, I'll likely lose all of those things anyway."

"Perhaps. But if you go now, it is a certainty. You've got a choice to make, Eliza. Stay with your family and fulfil your obligations or resign yourself to a lifetime of struggle and poverty. You've got less than an hour to decide which one it will be."

CHAPTER FOUR

Eliza felt frustration bubbling up inside her as she flung open the large French doors at the rear of Thistlewood House. If everything around her had not been so precious, she would have been tempted to break a vase or two. But that wouldn't have accomplished anything, and she knew it, so instead, she took a deep breath and headed for the one place she knew would calm her.

On her way up the staircase, she passed Melville and Cedric, who were walking in the other direction.

"Did you see him?" Cedric said to Melville, unaware of Eliza's presence.

"Yes, a handsome chap, if you're into that sort of thing."

"I wonder if—"

Just then, Cedric noticed his sister marching up the stairs.

"Did they tell you why you're here then, Liza?"

"Of all the nerve!" Eliza said, stopping two steps below her brothers.

"At least they care enough to match you to someone," Melville said. "I haven't been on so much as an evening walk with a woman in months."

"Well, that's a lie, Old Boy," Cedric said, pulling his pipe out from his waistcoat pocket. "They might just have you married off next, and to Anne Pilsbury no less."

"Anne Pilsbury!? I'd rather drink oil."

As furious as Eliza was, she couldn't help but smile at her brothers' banter. She had forgotten how much she missed that.

"You leave Anne Pilsbury alone, Melville," she said. "She's a lovely girl, I knew her when we were children."

"Too lovely!" Melville said, rubbing the front of his forehead with his hand.

"Oh, that's right," Cedric said, laughing. "Eliza doesn't know about your little dalliance with Anne at the Farmer's Dance."

"Oh, please, do tell." Eliza said, almost forgetting for a moment about her mother's ultimatum.

"Let's just say she had one too many glasses of Ruby Whitman's rum punch and cornered me while I was having a cigarette."

"Oh, methinks that Melville doth protest too much," Cedric said, popping his pipe in his mouth with a grin. "If I recall correctly, you were both found in the Whitman's prize Rhododendron bushes, and a little worse for wear I might add."

"She pushed me into them!" Melville insisted.

"I think you're right, Cedric," Eliza teased. "Mel, it's okay if you love her."

"I do not!" Melville insisted. "Right, you two absolute goons, I'm away for my afternoon walk."

"I'll come with you, Old Sport," Cedric said, following after him. "Can't have you being preyed upon by a Pilsbury!"

"He's right, Mel," Eliza added, looking down on her brother from above. "I hear Anne is a master of disguise, she could be waiting in any bush...Best stay away from Mother's rhododendrons!"

Left alone on the staircase, Eliza looked up at the pictures on the wall and wondered if her portrait would ever hang there. Probably not if she left. For once, rather than shirking under their disdainful gaze, Eliza gave them a good stare back.

There was something in the gesture that made Eliza feel better—more like herself than she had since arriving at Thistlewood—and as she neared the door to her childhood bedroom, she felt something akin to excitement.

Eliza grinned as she reached the door and pulled it open, eager to reconnect with this sacred space from her youth, but what she found inside was not what she expected. There, sitting on Eliza's old bed, was a young woman, barely twenty, her red hair striking against the black of her maid's uniform.

"Oh!" she said, jumping off the bed and onto her feet.

"Sorry...I didn't mean to intrude," Eliza said. It felt strange to apologize for entering her own room, but there was something about the look on the woman's face that made her feel like she was trespassing.

"I'm sorry, I shouldn't be here," the maid said. It was then that Eliza noticed the tears in her eyes.

Eliza felt a surge of empathy. Truth be told, she could have gone for a good cry at that moment too.

"Here," she said, taking a seat on the bed and patting the space beside her. "Why don't you sit down and tell me what's wrong?"

The maid sat down beside Eliza, but she did not answer her question. Instead, she wept uncontrollably.

"There, there, it's alright," Eliza said, putting her arm gently around the woman. "It's alright."

"Please don't tell Lady Montagu you found me in 'ere, Miss. This room belongs to her daughter, but bein' that she ain't here, it's the only unlocked place that no one goes."

"I won't say a word." Eliza said, moving her fingers across her mouth as though closing a zipper. "Now, tell me what's happened. Whatever it is, I'm sure we can find a way to solve the problem."

"There's no way out for this, Miss..." the maid said. She looked at Eliza, her bottom lip quivering, and Eliza could not help but notice the uncertainty in her eyes. The maid took a deep breath, seemingly deciding whether or not to reveal her secret, before uttering the phrase, "I'm pregnant..."

"Oh!" Eliza exclaimed. Her heart immediately went out to the maid. There was no wedding ring on her finger, no mark that would indicate one that had been recently removed. And while she was not personally one to judge a woman for falling pregnant out of wedlock, she knew the same could not be said about society at large—particularly at Thistlewood.

"I don't know what to do..."

"Does the father know?"

"No...I can't bear to tell him, Miss. Everythin' he had would be gone with the scandal. I can't be doin' that to him."

"I admire your loyalty, but he should know. Once you tell him, you can talk it out. Two heads are better than one."

In that moment, Eliza couldn't help but wish she had a person to talk her own problems out with. Her mother's ultimatum loomed large, and she was running out of time to make a decision.

"You look like you've got your own worries to follow, Miss?"

Eliza couldn't help but smile. Apparently, she wasn't nearly as good at hiding her feelings as she thought she was.

"I've been given an ultimatum by my family, Dear: Get married or be cut off."

Normally, Eliza would not have been so forthcoming, but she felt she could be honest with the maid. After all, the secret the maid had told her carried far greater risk.

"It's difficult to give up fancy things, isn't it, Miss?" the maid said, clearly referring to her own fears of being chased from Thistlewood House under the cloud of a scandal.

That insight hit Eliza hard. It was difficult to give up "fancy things" as she had put it. Eliza had talked the talk of someone casting aside the narrow views of class and gender superiority, but she had done so while living in the lap of luxury.

"Now," Eliza said, feeling a strange, spontaneous bond with the maid. "I'm supposed to meet a prospective partner, and if I do not 'meet my obligations' as Mother calls it, I'll be thrown into the streets."

"If you don't mind me sayin', Miss. I think you should hear this gentleman out. I come from poverty, and I ain't got no desire to go back if I can help it. I wouldn't want that for you either. What harm would it do to meet the man? Who knows? You might even like him."

What harm could it do? Eliza wondered.

"Well, I best be gettin' back. But thank you for your kindness," the maid said before wiping away a tear and heading for the door.

Eliza walking over to the window and looked across the estate, glorious and lushly green. The surrounding woodland was the ideal landscape for a painting, but there was no time for that. The evening dinner was looming on the horizon and Eliza's fate was hanging in the balance.

CHAPTER FIVE

Eliza took a deep breath as she stood at the top of the staircase. Wearing an emerald-green dinner dress, her hair tied up in a bejeweled hairpin, she looked every bit a respectable lady—aside from the striking red lipstick she had worn as a quiet act of rebellion. She was reasonably sure that even just the sight of it would give Great Aunt Martha a heart attack.

She could hear the servants below, chatting quietly. As she walked down the stairs, her anxiety rising and her heart pounding, she thought about her fellow suffragettes. She imagined them walking there beside her, looping their arms through hers as they descended into yet another hostile environment full of people with outdated thinking whose minds needed to be changed. Thinking of it that way made the evening more bearable. And thinking of them was enough to bring some confidence back to Eliza's stride.

Two servant boys with slicked back hair and white server jackets stood at the foot of the stairs, their jaws nearly scraping the floor.

"Careful," Eliza said as she fanned herself with an intricate cream-colored Chinese Brise fan, "if your mouths go any wider, my father is likely to mistake you for one of his hunting trophies and have you put up on the wall."

"Sorry, Miss," came the apology in unison.

"I'm just joshing," she said with a smile. "My name is Eliza. What are yours?"

They pointed at each other: "Frank and Willis, we're brothers."

"Frank, Willis, stick with me, boys. I don't go in for all this nonsense servant/master divide. But keep that under your aprons," she winked.

Neither of the boys knew how to take this, but they both beamed, their faces red.

"Please, this way, Miss." Frank said, as he and Willis led Eliza through the rear French doors and out into the garden.

"Ladies and gentlemen," came a booming voice from the side of the door. "Miss Eliza Montagu of Thistlewood House." The voice was Parkins, the family butler. He had been with the family since she was a little girl, and Eliza had always been very fond of him. She was delighted to see him again, and the feeling appeared to be mutual, as he broke decorum, just slightly, by slipping a gleeful smile in with his bow.

"Parkins! Know your place!" Great Aunt Martha chided as she walked furiously towards Eliza, wearing a cream gown which covered her from neck to feet. A plain tiara sat on top of her head, and Eliza almost laughed out loud when she realized just how much Great Aunt Martha looked like an illustration of the wicked snow queen from a story Cedric had read to her as a child.

Great Aunt Martha's face was wrinkled with more than time. She frowned at everyone, except during events such as these when important guests were present. In those instances, she usually kept an unsettling smile upon her face, one that reminded Eliza of the Kabuki masks she had seen in Japan.

"Smile my dear," Great Aunt Martha hissed at Eliza, as she waved at the guests who were standing near the dining table. "And don't make a mess of things. Lord Darlington will make this family three times as rich if you aren't dunce enough to ruin it."

Eliza smiled at the guests and let out a little wave, whispering to Great Aunt Martha through gritted teeth.

"I'll do my best to not embarrass you, Great Aunt Martha. Could you afford me the same courtesy?"

Rather than engage with Eliza, Great Aunt Martha huffed and puffed and then walked back to the guests to avoid a scene.

"Don't go too hard on the old Dear," said Cedric quietly. "One of these days she's going to get so mad that she'll just disappear in a puff of smoke."

"Where are Melville and Mercy?" Eliza asked. "I could use some reinforcements."

"Mercy is over there, enthralled by one of the Darlington's cousins. Melville, on the other hand, well I have no idea where—"

As if in reply, Melville entered the marquee, still struggling with his bow tie.

"Come here," Eliza said, ushering him over and quickly fixing his tie before Great Aunt Martha or anyone else could chastise him for it. She knew how it felt to be on the receiving end of their disapproval.

"Where were you?" Cedric asked.

"Just taking care of something…So these are the Darlingtons?" Cedric asked, gesturing towards the family by the dining room table. "And of course, we know the Fairfaxes, don't we, Liza?"

"Enough of that." Eliza said, although she did know the Fairfaxes. One of them all too well.

"Be on your best behavior, Melville," Cedric interjected. "Watch how much you're drinking."

"Have I ever embarrassed either of you before?"

"Yes," Eliza and Cedric said in unison.

Just then, a server came over with a tray of wide-brimmed crystal champagne glasses.

"Oh! Champagne!" Melville said, excitedly.

Eliza immediately recognized the server. It was the maid who had confided in her earlier in the day about her pregnancy. Eliza smiled at her, but the maid tried her best not to make it obvious that they were already acquainted.

Melville took a glass and raised it.

"Here's to my sister and her triumphant return to Thistlewood."

"Here, here!" Mercy said loudly from across the room before being chastised by their mother for raising her voice.

Cedric and Eliza clinked glasses with Melville, but Eliza's attention was drawn to the maid. The color had run from her face. She was obviously shocked that she had confided in one of the Montagus, afraid that her secret would get out. While Cedric and Melville were ribbing each other about what they were wearing, Eliza mouthed *it's okay* to the girl, who smiled nervously before returning to the small serving station in the corner.

"Ladies and Gentlemen!" boomed Parkins again. "Please be seated. Dinner is about to be served."

Lady Montagu took Eliza's arm in a way that would have appeared gentle to the untrained eye but, in reality, was anything but and guided her to a seat halfway down the table. Eliza had hoped that she would be sitting with her family, but instead, she was surrounded by strangers. On one side, a handsome man in his early thirties, dressed in an exquisitely tailored dinner suit with diamond cufflinks. On the other side, an elderly lady, who Eliza guessed was the man's mother.

"I'm Lord Darlington," the man said as Eliza took a seat beside him. "Do I have the honor of meeting Miss Eliza Montagu?"

"Yes...Pleased to meet you."

Eliza offered her hand, which he took, before kissing the back of it like an old aristocrat from the Romantic Era. Eliza found the gesture tiresome. She found him tiresome, but she made polite conversation anyway.

"And where are you from, Lord Darlington?" she asked.

"Darlington."

On hearing this, Melville let out a raucous laugh from down the table.

"Quiet, Melville," snapped Lady Montagu, her stare more than enough to silence her son's humor.

Parkins arrived at the table with the servers, who placed the first starter before each guest.

"Veal for a starter?" Lord Darlington said. "I would have thought it better for a main course, no?"

"Eh..." stammered Lord Montagu. "Quite right. But the cook insisted, and he is such a marvelous chap. French, you know. Came here from Paris..."

"You're babbling, Dear," Eliza's mother said loud enough for most to hear.

"I've always found the idea of having set courses a tad strange. I wouldn't mind eating my dessert first, that way I'd know there was always room left for it!" Eliza joked.

Melville laughed. Cedric laughed. But Lord Darlington wore a puzzled expression on his face, and now the entire table was listening to their conversation.

"I'm sure, Miss Montagu," he began, "that you understand and appreciate the importance of ceremony?"

"Of course she does!" Great Aunt Martha insisted a little too quickly. Eliza knew she should stop talking, but, well, being silent was never her strong suite.

"Well..." she said, looking around the table. "It doesn't really matter, does it? I mean, ceremony is ceremony, but it doesn't really mean anything in the end."

"Doesn't mean anything? Miss Montagu, it is through ceremony and tradition that the world is shaped. Otherwise, how would we tell the difference between ourselves and the Help?"

Eliza felt her pulse begin to quicken. Much like with the man at the suffragette march, she could not let this wrong-headed thinking go unresponded to.

"I see...So, what you are saying is that we need ceremony to show who is better than whom?"

"It is not just who is better, Miss Montagu. It's about who belongs where. I'm sure they are all decent people, but come now, can they build empires? Can they negotiate treaties? Can they navigate the complexities of the marketplace? Of course not. And I am sure they would agree that staying in their place is far better than embarrassing themselves by trying to join a class they simply cannot keep up with."

A few people clapped at the table. Others nodded in agreement. But Eliza was enraged.

This, she thought, *is exactly why I left this place. And this is precisely the reason I should not have come back.*

"Well spoken, Sir," Lord Montagu said, standing up. "But enough of our digressions. Here's a toast to the Darlingtons for coming all this way and—"

Eliza knew her father was just trying to change the subject and keep the peace, but she could not help feeling wildly disappointed in him. What Darlington had said was abhorrent, and while her father may not have had enough backbone to say so, she certainly did.

"I won't raise my glass to that sort of antiquated, pompous, primitive ideology!" she said loudly.

Melville, who was at least three drinks ahead of everyone else, burst into laughter. Unfortunately, no one else shared Melville's good humor.

"Please excuse Eliza, Lord Darlington," Great Aunt Martha begged. "She has been away from our good home for some time and has picked up some bad habits from her suffragette friends in the Great City."

"Oh, dear," Lord Darlington's mother said. "She isn't one of those ruffians, surely?"

"Those ruffians," Eliza retorted, "are the future of this country."

"Eliza, please..." Lady Montagu said, her face flushed with embarrassment.

"I have to say that I find the entire Suffragette movement to be ungrateful," Lord Darlington said.

"The suffragettes are courageous campaigners, ensuring that a decent and free society can be enjoyed by all and that everyone—whether they are young or old, male or female, rich or poor—will have a voice and can democratically elect to power those who believe in real change. It's easy for all of us sitting here, being waited on by good people who are not beneath us—"

At that, a collective gasp arose from the table.

"—These are the people who served in the war, who keep our hospitals running, and who fight every day just to survive. They have equal value to you and I, Lord Darlington. In fact, as I look upon you now, I see that each of them has more value in their smallest finger than you have in your whole body!"

"Is this the way you speak to your guests here at Thistlewood!?" Lord Darlington demanded, glaring at Lord Montagu. But before Lord Montagu could answer, a loud clapping sound rose up from the other end of the table.

"Spoken like a true Londoner," a suave voice said.

Eliza recognized the voice instantly, and she was floored by the realization. Oliver Fairfax was there. He had been there the whole time, sat at the opposite end of the table, obscured from her view by the person sitting next to him. She could hardly believe she hadn't seen him sooner, though, admittedly, it was an excessively long, full table. Plus, her mother's ultimatum had her more than a little distracted.

"If you were all as interested in being good people as you are in what we're having for a starter, this world would be a much better place," Oliver said, smiling across the table at Eliza. "Tell me, Miss Montagu. Would you care to grab a little air with me before we enjoy the main course?"

"I would be delighted."

Oliver stood up, walked around to Eliza, and offered her his arm. He was tall, strong, and with his slicked back blond hair and effortless smile, he was the absolute antithesis of Lord Darlington. Eliza often found herself getting lost just looking at him, and this moment was no exception.

Eliza took his arm, and together, the two walked out of the marquee. Eliza knew she should have been worrying about the consequences of what had just happened, but she couldn't focus on that. Not now. Now, she was too busy thinking about the unexpected appearance of Oliver Fairfax and trying to figure out what he might do next.

CHAPTER SIX

"You really are a rotter!" Eliza said as Oliver Fairfax led her by the arm away from Thistlewood House. It loomed behind them in the blue hue of the moon, and with each step, the noise of shocked chatter from the marquee lessened into a momentary dream behind them.

"Me! Whatever do you mean?" Oliver asked, a smile spreading across his face. Oliver had always had the sort of smile you could get lost in—something Eliza, herself, had done many times before. That was the problem.

"You know fine well. You should have told me you were coming here. At least you could have warned me about what I was walking into."

Oliver patted Eliza's hand on his arm.

"And ruin all my fun? You know I had to see what fireworks would go off. There's very little entertainment these days. Everyone is so damned serious."

Eliza wanted to sigh, but she didn't. Instead, she looked across the pristine lawn in the moonlight and laughed. There was no changing Ollie. There never would be.

Eliza had known Oliver since they were children. Growing up, they had been friends, running around the estate together and getting into mischief as they played in the garden. As teenagers, there had been moments—moonlit walks or tipsy trips to her father's wine cellar where they drank whiskey and chatted or danced—where Eliza thought maybe, just maybe, this was a man worth settling down for.

But Ollie wasn't the sort to settle down—or at least, if he was, he'd never expressed any interest in doing it with Eliza. And frankly, in some ways, Eliza was relieved by that. She was increasingly unconvinced that she was the marrying kind, and regardless, she found that she wanted to shake Oliver every bit as often as she wanted to kiss him.

But still, there was something in the way he looked at her that made Eliza think twice.

"I haven't seen you in London for a while. Is this where you've been hiding out?"

"I grew tired of London, Liza."

"Or did London grow tired of you?" Eliza asked with a laugh. "What sort of trouble did you get into this time?"

"None," Ollie answered, this time his words more serious. "I grew tired of all the buzz, you know? People always moving around. The dances, the lunches, the endless dinners…And you with your Suffragette movement. So, I thought, why not spend the summer in the countryside where we grew up? I've been renting a little place in Winchester. A cottage in fact."

"You and the quiet life? Why do I think there's more to it than that?"

"You can think what you like, Old Girl."

"I hardly think I qualify as old. I'm two years younger than you!"

"And you seem it," he said.

Ollie always had a way of hurting Eliza. Even with the smallest row, he could form his words into a dagger. Eliza hid the hurt. She always did that. There would be no showing weakness from her, even if, deep down, she was wounded.

"Did you know about this Darlington business? Mother wants me to marry the man."

"And will you?"

"Would you care?"

Ollie did not answer. He always danced around the topic of Eliza's feelings and, even more so, his own.

"Maybe I will…" Eliza said, hoping to get a reaction out of him. But the one she received was not at all the one she had hoped for.

"Maybe you should. Lots of money and prestige with that family. You could do a lot worse, Old Girl."

"What is it with you!?" Eliza raised her voice in exasperation. "Can't you see that—"

Before Eliza could finish, a voice as shrill as the night stretched across the moonlit lawn.

"Eliza Montagu! Oliver Fairfax! Get back here this instant!" Great Aunt Martha commanded, her aging figure dimly marching in their direction from afar.

"Are you sure Old Martha isn't the ghost of Thistlewood? She does look a bit like a haggard specter."

As Eliza laughed at Ollie's joke, Great Aunt Martha focused in on where they were standing, marching with greater force than before and echoing:

"Eliza! Oliver! You will not embarrass this family tonight!"

30

"Be a good lad and run interference for me, won't you?" Eliza said, slapping Ollie on the back like a playground chum.

"You're not coming back to the dinner? Are you sure that's wise?"

"I don't know," replied Eliza as she backed away. "I might come back, but if I do, it will be in my own time. Not dragged in by the ear like I'm eight years old…Ta, ta for now!"

The truth was Eliza knew that it wasn't wise. She knew there would be consequences for her actions, and the thought of that lodged a pit in her stomach. But she couldn't help it. She simply could not bring herself to walk back into that marquee. Not yet, anyway.

"Eliza! Wait!" Ollie groaned with a whisper, but it was too late. Eliza had disappeared off into the night and across the lawn out of view, and Great Aunt Martha was now bearing down on him, ready to give him an earful.

Eliza watched from behind a hedgerow as Great Aunt Martha disappeared with Ollie back towards the marquee. She could almost hear her great aunt's seething words, but she couldn't quite make them out. That was probably for the best.

Eliza's decided to stretch her legs for a few minutes with a walk on the grounds before going back to the marquee, but the night had other plans for her. As she started walking, she heard a strange sound. It was soft and subtle at first, but then it leapt out of the darkness and echoed around the grounds. It was a sound Eliza could not ignore, no matter how much her further tardiness would enrage her family.

It was a sound that needed investigation.

It was the helpless plea of something or someone in pain.

Eliza moved in the opposite direction of Thistlewood House. Though it was dark and there were no electrified lights like those she had become accustomed to on the streets of London, a childhood spent on these grounds had taught her how to let the moon and stars guide her.

The grass felt soft beneath her shoes, and the lavender in the air was now overpowered by a stronger scent—one that Eliza knew all too well. She had followed that same, musty smell of hay many times as a child. Her father housed a number of animals in the stables, and Eliza used to spend hours there petting and talking to them. Often, Eliza felt a greater affinity for horses and dogs than people, and her father, being the old softy that he was, was often happy to oblige those feelings by buying her a pet or two.

The sound came again. This time it was closer. The sound wore on Eliza, and she picked up the pace. She could not stand for anyone or anything to be in pain.

Up ahead, a dark, rectangular shape came into view, and from it a small ray of candlelight filtered through a half-opened wooden shutter.

"Someone is in the stable," she whispered to herself.

Eliza was nearly sprinting now. She knew her Great Aunt Martha would have a fit if she saw her doing such a thing, but she did not care. Whatever was happening in that stable, Eliza had to stop it. And she had to stop it now.

As she finally reached the cold, mossy stone of the building, she slowed to a halt. She wasn't sure what was happening inside, but she was certain that she did not want to lose the advantage provided by the element of surprise.

Methodically, she tiptoed through the darkness, moving slowly and carefully until she was just inches from the window.

"Blast you to hell!" a voice shouted from inside.

Though she could not yet see the person who was doing the screaming, Eliza did not need to see him to know he was drunk. His words were slurred and slow, but the alcohol had clearly done nothing to dull his rage.

A drunkard is capable of anything, Eliza thought, as she stood on her tiptoes in an effort to get a better look. Unfortunately, the darkness made it impossible to decipher much of what was happening. All Eliza could see was a shadowy figure, stumbling back and forth—something in his hand, though she could not identify what.

Suddenly, another sound cut through the night, joining the chorus of cries that had brought Eliza here in the first place. There was the sound of something being thrown, followed by the sound of glass, shattering.

Danger be damned. She had to get in there.

Eliza knew what she was doing was dangerous, but she did not care. What was the point of being alive if not to use our time, energy, and wits to help each other?

The pained cry rose up again, cutting through the inky blackness, spurring Eliza on—telling her to move faster. She rushed around the side of the building and threw open a wooden door.

It was dark, and all Eliza could see at the moment was the straw-filled interior directly in front of her. Careful to make as little noise as possible, she made her way across the barn to where the drunkard was standing, belt in hand. He wielded it like a weapon, and Eliza could tell he was only moments away from bringing it down on the shadowy figure in front of him.

"Stop!" Eliza cried.

She knew, as soon as she'd done it, how foolish that was. He wasn't going to stop simply because she told him too, and now he knew she was there. Rather than saving the object of his rage, she had simply put herself in danger too. Her belief in the stupidity of that split-second decision was only further confirmed as the man turned and stared at her—his bleary eyes filled with rage and the belt in his hand.

CHAPTER SEVEN

Before her was the stocky figure of a man in black and white servant clothes. He was clean shaven, and his hair was slicked back. His bloodshot eyes took a moment to focus on Eliza.

"Don't you dare!" Eliza yelled. "I'm a lady of Thistlewood. You stop this, immediately!" She hated using her inherited title, but given that the man was a servant, she believed he would be more open to abiding by her words if he knew who she was. Plus, it wasn't like she had any other way to stop him.

The man stumbled backwards with a confused look on his face and then his heel caught in the ground. Falling over, he landed on a large pile of hay. Beside him, the clink of a bottle rolling on the floor sounded.

He smiled as though he had discovered a great lost treasure.

"There ye' are, ye wee blighter!" He said as he stretched over the hay, grabbed the bottle, and took a swig."

Eliza recognized it as coming from her father's extensive Cognac collection. She would have said something about it then, but there were more pressing matters at hand: like finding the source of the crying Eliza had heard earlier. She scanned the barn in search of the source and was surprised to find not a person, but a small brown hound with large, pleading eyes.

"Beating one of my father's bloodhounds and stealing his alcohol?"

"Out of my way, Miss," the man said angrily. "Let me teach this pup a thing or two!"

The dog cowered in anticipation of the strike, but the hit did not come. Eliza stopped it by lurching forward and putting herself between the dog and its attacker.

The man let out a sigh. "Please, Miss. I'm havin' a bad day."

"No matter how bad your day is going, it cannot justify cruelty to a little sweetheart like this."

Eliza moved across the floor carefully before kneeling down in front of the cowering dog. Its brown coat with a white underbelly was vibrating with fear.

"It's okay," Eliza said in a friendly tone. "It's okay…"

Eliza slowly raised her hand and began to pat the dog gently on the head. At first, the animal was tense and reluctant, but it quickly seemed to realize that Eliza was there to help. At the very least, her affection was a counterpoint to the servant's rough hand.

As Eliza patted the animal gingerly, she found herself filled with compassion for the poor thing. But she also found herself filled with rage at the fact that someone could treat a poor, defenseless animal that way.

"What's to become of this little one?" she asked, pointing to the dog cowering at her feet.

"He's too little for the hunt, Miss. He's to be sent to a mill."

"A dog mill?" Eliza asked, surprised. "Absolutely not!"

Eliza had heard about what happened to dogs in those mills, and there was no scenario in which she was going to allow that to be the fate that awaited this dog. He'd been through enough already.

There were several leashes hanging on a nearby post, and Eliza marched over and grabbed one immediately. She bent down and placed the leash gently around the dog's neck as he shivered anxiously.

"Miss, you can't!"

"If you think this little one is going to be sent to a mill for breeding and kept in a cage for the rest of his life, you have another think coming!" Eliza declared as she walked confidently back into the night, the little dog following obediently behind her, and the man standing stunned in the doorway, his mouth gaping open in drunken shock.

"Of all the things, Little One," Eliza said as she walked back across the pristine grass to Thistlewood House. "We'll find a good home for you, don't you worry."

The dog whined but kept close to Eliza, seemingly caught between uncertainty and trust. And then suddenly, Eliza noticed another noise. She listened closely, trying to decipher precisely what it was. As she continued walking, it became clear that what she was hearing were voices, though she could not quite decipher who they belonged to or what they were saying. She could, however, tell that they were rapidly coming closer.

She stashed herself behind a nearby statue, pleased to see the little hound had followed her lead and seemed to understand the need for discretion. Together, they watched as a dark, shadowy figure cut through the grounds and headed towards the marquee.

How odd, Eliza thought. It wasn't unusual to see people around the estate, but it was awfully late for them to be just roaming around the grounds. Though, as a person doing exactly the same thing, she was hardly in a position to judge.

The dog tugged gently on the leash once the figure passed, but Eliza didn't move. She had distinctly heard two voices, and she didn't want to move until both of the people had passed. While Eliza could not make out the words they had been saying, she could tell by their tones that the conversation was intense, and she did not want them thinking they had been eavesdropped on.

Eventually, however, she had to admit that waiting might not be prudent. Perhaps the other person wasn't coming or had left a different way, but whatever the case, Eliza had been standing here for at least five minutes, and she was late already. If she didn't leave soon, dinner would be over, and the choice of whether or not to go back would be made for her.

Quietly, she stepped out from behind the statue and, much to her surprise, directly into the oncoming path of what Eliza imagined was the owner of the second voice. She squinted her eyes, peering into the moonlight in an effort to decipher the image. As she got closer, things started to take shape, and Eliza soon realized the person in front of her was none other than the servant girl she had comforted a few hours prior.

"Hello!" Eliza said, pleasantly surprised by the unexpected turn of events, but also concerned for the young woman's wellbeing.

"Hello, miss."

"Are you alright? Do you—"

"I'm sorry, Miss" she interjected. "But I must be goin'. I'm needed in the kitchen at once."

"Of course," Eliza said as the young woman hurried off.

Eliza believed the maid about being needed in the kitchen, but there was something strange about the conversation—a feeling that was only accentuated by the fact that the maid never once looked her in the eye.

The dog at her feet whined quietly, pulling Eliza out of her thoughts and into the present.

"Right you are, little one. We must be going."

Together, Eliza and the hound walked past a high row of bushes that loomed in the darkness at the front of the manor and up the stone steps. They were halfway to the landing when she heard a voice from the open doorway ahead.

"Nice little hound. Is he yours?" Darlington asked. He was standing in his pristine dinner suit, leaning against the doorframe and smoking a pipe.

"No…Yes…I don't know," Eliza said, annoyed by both his sudden presence and the fact that he felt he had a right to ask her anything about her life at this point. "Aren't you supposed to be having dinner."

"There was some mix up in the kitchen. Seems the next course is taking longer than previously thought."

Eliza laughed.

"Mother and Aunt Martha will have a fit."

"Indeed. Not becoming of a place like Thistlewood at all."

Eliza sighed at Darlington's pompous attitude, but after giving the stable hand an earful, she was in no mood for another verbal fencing match with the Lord, so instead, she simply rolled her eyes and tried to walk past him through the doorway.

As she did, Darlington reached out and grabbed her arm.

"Do you mind?!" Eliza exclaimed, looking down at his hand.

"I'm sorry, Eliza," Darlington said, releasing his grip. "But I thought it would be good for us to have a chat before going back to the marquee. You know, for what it's worth, I'm really not as bad as you think."

"Is that so?" Eliza said skeptically, folding her arms in front of her chest.

"I am a man of business, Eliza. I have to keep up pretenses to a degree, to take care of my family. But I'm not as old-fashioned as I appear. I would like the chance to show you that. Perhaps over a quiet drink somewhere for a little while after dinner? A conversation? Would you grant me that?"

There was something in the way he spoke to her now—a sincerity that made her believe him. And if what he was saying was true, she felt genuinely sorry for him.

"Were you forced into this too?"

Darlington looked around as if checking to see if anyone else was listening.

"Yes, I was. But I wouldn't mind making the most of it. You…Interest me, Eliza. You're not like the sort of upper-class women Mother tends to try and partner me with."

"Partner?" Eliza said. "Sounds more like a business merger."

"Sometimes…But business can be pleasurable. It can even be fun." Darlington looked down at his shining black, leather shoes for a moment, and his shoulder hunched. For just a moment, he lost much of the bravado she had initially seen in him. She liked him much better this way.

"I know you went for a walk with Oliver Fairfax, but how about just one drink with me after the party? We might see eye-to-eye on more than you think."

"I'll consider it," she said.

"Please, Eliza. Just give me a chance. Perhaps there is a way for us to both get everything we want. At the very least, I'd like to try and find out."

For the first time, Eliza saw something in Darlington. A spark. A glimmer of something worthwhile.

Ollie isn't interested, so why the hell not? she thought.

"Okay," she said. "But only one drink."

Darlington's face lit up.

"I look forward to it, Eliza."

Eliza found herself unexpectedly smiling at Darlington. There was something in his demeanor that she found pleasantly disarming. If she stayed out here, she might actually fall for the fellow, and she couldn't have that. It would give her mother far too much satisfaction.

"I must take this little one somewhere. Will you make me a Martini?" Eliza asked.

"Of course. See you at the marquee?" Darlington asked, delighted.

"See you there."

Lord Darlington walked off back into the house and to the rear exit, just as Parkins's booming voice called out:

"Dinner is served!"

Eliza picked up the pace. Her mother had been very clear about the consequences of missing dinner, and if she was going to endure them, she wanted it to be because she was making a stand—not because she lollygagged too long on her way to find a hiding place for the dog.

Thankfully, she quickly stumbled on Frank and asked him to take the dog to a quiet room and make sure it was watered and fed. He obliged, of course, but as he led the dog away from Eliza, it began to whine and cry unbearably.

Eliza knew it would cause a storm with her family, but she could not leave the poor little thing on its own like that. So, she accompanied Frank and the dog into a small, unused bedroom on the ground floor, where she sat by the fireplace and soothed him until Frank brought some water and food to the room.

Once the dog finally settled, she got up and began the trek to the marquee. The moonlight from outside cast its dim light through rows of large, ornate windows as Eliza moved along the polished marble floor of a small reception area that had not been used in many years. In the distance, she could hear the merriment being had at the marquee. Her sister's gleeful laugh floated in on the summer breeze, which came as no surprise to Eliza. She'd always loved a good dinner party. What did surprise Eliza, however, was the other sound she heard moving through the house.

Somewhere nearby, there were footsteps, which caught Eliza off guard. There wasn't supposed to be anyone in this part of the house at this time of night. In fact, she had very deliberately chosen that location for the dog for precisely that reason.

All of the guests were at the marquee, so it wasn't as though someone had simply wandered off and unexpectedly gotten lost in this portion of the estate. The servants were all occupied. If someone was here, they were making a very intentional decision to be somewhere they weren't supposed to, and Eliza could not help but wonder if that meant something nefarious was afoot.

She tried to convince herself that perhaps she hadn't heard footsteps at all but rather something else entirely, but the sound was unmistakable. Someone was there. And they were headed right for her.

CHAPTER EIGHT

Eliza turned a brass knob on the wall next to her, and the row of gaslights reaching across the long corridor flickered, providing just enough light for her to see the source of the footsteps. There was a man at the other end of the corridor; Of that, Eliza was sure. But which man remained a mystery. He disappeared through the blackness of an open doorway before Eliza could make out his features.

Eliza felt a cold chill creep up her spine. She wasn't usually someone who was easily spooked, and she'd rarely ever felt fear while exploring the halls of Thistlewood, but there was something about the man's presence that made her pulse quicken and her hands start to shake.

"Who is that?" she whispered to herself.

There was only one way to find out, and, despite the sinking feeling in her stomach, Eliza was never the type to shirk away from a mystery. Her curiosity and determination had always been greater than her fear. So, as she had when she was getting ready to face the hecklers at the march in London, Eliza steadied her nerves and strode against the darkness and uncertainty.

When she reached the doorway the figure had disappeared into, she was met with a cross section of passageways. Looking forward, she saw nothing but the dim gaslights trailing off into the distance. They had been left on in case any of the guests wanted to be escorted around the house.

What a waste of gas and money, Eliza thought as she scanned the area.

To the right, she saw a similar scene, so she turned her gaze to the left. As she did, she saw the grey outline of a man disappearing into a large doorway.

"Hello?" Eliza said loudly. She was certain the man had heard her, but he did not answer.

Swallowing her nerves, Eliza marched down the hallway to another large doorway. It was decorated with ornate, polished brass trim around the edges, and Eliza recognized it immediately. It led to a place she had frequently hidden as a child. Growing up, it had been a special place to her—one where she always felt safe—but now, in the dim gaslight, with the sound of some strange man skulking about, it took on a more ominous appearance.

As Eliza stepped across the threshold, she noted the change in the air. It was humid in a way that the rest of the house was not. Once inside, she found herself surrounded by a sea of exotic plants, some small and some stretching all the way to the top of the high, glass ceiling.

The room she now found herself in was a large conservatory, an unexpected piece of exotic land right there in the countryside of merry old England. Several palm trees were dotted around, and there was a small pond in the center of the room. Paths darted off in three directions, giving the impression that the space was larger and more labyrinthine than it actually was. The bushy leaves and reeds of the room felt like a world away from the dinner suits of the marquee, and Eliza found herself wanting to get lost in it—to hide here, safe and sound, as she had as a child.

But that was not to be. After all, she had a dinner to attend—and before that, a mystery to solve.

Despite her best efforts, Eliza could not see the strange figure who had walked into the room just moments before, likely because the paths were obscured by overhanging tree leaves in full bloom.

Still, Eliza could sense that someone was there.

"Hello?" Eliza called. She was trying to sound confident and calm, but she couldn't help noticing the hint of nerves that had creeped into the edges of her voice.

"Yes?"

Eliza's pulse quickened.

"I'm sorry, I can't see you," Eliza said. "I was just wondering if you needed help getting back to the marquee. It's easy to get lost in this old house. I grew up here, and even I sometimes get turned around."

"I am not a dinner guest."

Suddenly, there was a rustle of leaves, and the owner of the voice—a man in his forties with a bald head—came into view. He was smartly dressed in an evening suit.

"I am sorry if I startled you," he said quietly before extending his hand to her and saying "I'm—"

"Barnsley?"

He nodded as Eliza reached out and shook his hand.

"I think I saw you when I arrived earlier. Father says you're an old friend."

41

"Yes, your father has been very kind to allow me to stay here while I recuperate."

His voice had all the precision of the officer class, but there was something about him that made Eliza doubt the veracity of his words. She studied the man closely, trying to determine what exactly it was that made her doubt him. As she did, she noticed a small notepad in his left hand.

"What's that?" she asked.

Barnsley looked down at it sheepishly.

"Oh, it's nothing, I just…tend to note my thoughts down whenever I can."

Barnsley quickly slipped the notepad into the inner pocket of his dinner suit jacket, but not before Eliza saw some scribblings. It looked more like numbers than a man's deepest thoughts, though there were words attached.

"I'm Eliza Montagu," Eliza offered.

"Yes, I have seen portraits of you in one of the upper halls."

"Do you like the conservatory?" Eliza asked. "I've always found it calming."

Barnsley nodded. Eliza wasn't sure why she felt compelled to make conversation with the man. After all, there was a dinner she urgently needed to get to, and she was already late. Plus, he wasn't exactly a sparkling conversationalist.

Still, there was something about him that Eliza couldn't quite put her finger on, and she hoped that talking to him would help her figure out what it was.

"Yes," Barnsley replied. "It is good to be in nature. The grounds are most excellent here at Thistlewood House, though truth be told, I prefer it here. Being around these colonial plants is a reminder of better days."

"Father said you served during the war…You must have seen terrible things."

As soon as the words had left her mouth, she regretted them. They were excessively forthright, even by Eliza's standards.

"I…I'm sorry to pry…My parents always said my curiosity would get the better of me."

"Not at all," he said. "I find it refreshing. Most here seem to be intent on maintaining a façade of gentility when the world needs more who are willing to be so direct."

Eliza was about to respond when, suddenly, she heard the sound of more footsteps coming down the hall. And this time, she knew exactly who they belonged to.

"I better be going," Eliza said hurriedly. "I hope you feel better."

"Thank you, Miss Montagu. Once I finish my thoughts in my notebook, I think I'll be quite satisfied."

Eliza found these words odd. There was something in them. If she had to bet on it, there was a double meaning in there, but before she could ask what that meaning was, the footsteps got so loud and so close that even Barnsley noticed.

"Trouble?" Barnsley asked.

"Always."

"Eliza Montagu!"

Lady Montagu had not even entered the glasshouse yet, but her shrill voice bounced down the corridor and into the conservatory regardless.

"That will be my mother," Eliza said quietly, before raising her voice. "In the glasshouse, Mother!"

It only took a moment before Lady Montagu materialized in front of them like an angry apparition, bristling and red-faced.

"Does it please you to exhaust your poor mother!" she said. "One of the servant boys said you were in this wing. Something about taking care of a dog no less. Am I to believe you value animals more than your own family?"

"It depends on which member of the family you're referring to."

Barnsley laughed at that, catching Lady Montagu entirely off guard.

"I did not see you there, Mr. Barnsley."

If Eliza didn't know any better, she would have thought her mother was rattled. But that was not possible. Lady Montagu did not believe in being rattled. She could stand in the center of a hurricane with nary a hair out of place.

"I was having a delightful conversation with your daughter, Lady Montagu. Quite delightful."

What followed was one of the most unexpected interactions Eliza had ever had with her mother. With anyone, really.

Rather than yelling at her, threatening her, or grabbing her by the arm and pulling her to the marquee, Lady Montagu stepped forward and gently placed her hand on her daughter's shoulder.

"Come, Child. Please."

Eliza had rarely seen such softness from her mother. It was disarming.

"Yes, Mother," she said. She felt strangely subservient—a posture she never adopted with her mother—but it felt like the appropriate response to her mother's strange change in tact.

"I trust you have everything you need, Mr. Barnsley?" Lady Montagu said.

"If I don't, you'll be the first to know."

"Good night, Mr. Barnsley," Eliza said.

"Goodnight, Eliza," he replied, though Eliza could barely hear him, as her mother had already started ushering her swiftly out of the room.

There was an urgency in her mother's footsteps that frightened Eliza. There was an anxiousness here that went beyond the need to simply return to the dinner party. Her mother wasn't rushing to something, she was rushing away from something—something she seemed to genuinely fear. It was the fear that frightened Eliza. Being brave was the one thing she and her mother had in common. Lady Montagu never feared anything. Not like that.

Eliza wasn't sure what was going on. She did not know what had frightened her mother. But she knew one thing for certain: Something must be very, very wrong.

CHAPTER NINE

As Eliza walked out through the rear French doors, the marquee came into view once more. Her mother, who continued walking alongside her, had barely uttered a word since they left Barnsley in the green house, and her silence was utterly unnerving. There would be a confrontation once the dinner party was over, of that there was no doubt. Eliza just hoped she could successfully get through the rest of the evening while straddling the line between staying true to herself and not fighting with anyone.

As she approached the open doorway to the marquee, she could hear the busy murmur of conversation, and the rich smell of tobacco, most of it cigar smoke, filled the air. This Eliza knew to be a certain sign that all courses were finished, and the guests were now enjoying themselves. No one, not even Melville, was rude enough to start smoking at the dinner table.

The dining table was being removed by a group of servants, two of whom were Frank and Willis, the brothers Eliza had spoken with earlier on the stairwell. One nudged the other slightly, and they both smiled at Eliza, who nodded politely in return.

"Eyes straight, Boys," Eliza heard Parkins whisper the moment he caught their brief violation of decorum.

"Miss, would you do me the honor of allowing me to escort you to your seat?" Parkins asked. This was not exactly etiquette, but ever since she was small, Parkins had always looked out for Eliza. She was grateful to see that her time away had not changed that.

"Indeed, Parkins. Thank you."

Parkins put out his arm, which Eliza took readily, and guided her towards the rear of the marquee where a large number of armchairs had been arranged. On one side, the men were talking and enjoying their cigars; on the other, the ladies of the evening were sipping sherry and chattering away.

"Everything will be okay, Miss," Parkins said under his breath.

Eliza did not reply, but she did squeeze his arm to let him know how much she appreciated his kind words.

"Ah, at last," sniped Great Aunt Martha. "Glad to see you've come to your senses! Come and sit with me and Lady Darlington."

"I was thinking of joining the men, actually."

Before Great Aunt Martha could quell her horror long enough to formulate a reprimand, a young man sitting next to Lord Darlington stood up. His hair was a deep red, and he had an enthusiastic way about him which immediately charmed Eliza.

"Indeed, you would be welcome!" he said before extending his hand to Eliza. She took it and was pleasantly surprised by his decision to shake, rather than kiss, it.

"My name is Jacob."

"Eliza," she said. "Delighted to meet you."

"I'm terribly sorry I didn't have a chance to introduce myself earlier. Unfortunately," he said, waving towards Lord Darlington, "I'm one of those stuffy Darlingtons."

"I heard your speech earlier tonight," he said quietly to Eliza. "I found it bang on the money."

"Forgive my brother," Lord Darlington said, rising with a smile from his armchair. "Jacob is a little less refined at the edges."

"I like less refined," Eliza said, smiling at Jacob before turning back towards his older brother. "How was your meal, Lord Darlington? I hope I didn't detain you from it earlier?"

"To be detained by you was a pleasure..."

"Oh dear, Charlie, that doesn't sound so refined," Jacob retorted, his joke eliciting a small rustle of laughter in those close enough to hear it.

"I would so enjoy speaking again later if possible, Miss Montagu."

But before she could answer, Cedric appeared, holding two glasses of champagne.

"There you are, Liza," he said as he handed her a glass. "Some champagne for the girl of the hour."

"Thanks. Where's Mel?"

"I have no idea. He's been dipping in and out. You know what he's like. Probably has a stash of gin in his room and is trying to get a card game going."

"A card game! Now that would liven things up a bit," Jacob said.

"Be careful, Melville is a bit of a shark when it comes to parlor games," Eliza said with a grin. "Cedric once lost his shoes to him during a holiday, and Mel insisted he walk all the way home without them.

Cedric groaned at the memory. "All four miles."

"So, Cedric," Jacob said with a grin. "Any embarrassing stories about your sister here? If she's to be my sister-in-law—"

"—As always, you're premature," Lord Darlington interrupted.

"Not at all!" It was clear Jacob had had a few drinks, and the Martini glass in his hand swirled around half full and ready to spill with each gesture. "Eliza's mother already has you two married off."

"I'd like to think I might have a say in that," Eliza said. It was the least inflammatory thing she could think of to say, though she knew full well her mother and Great Aunt Martha would strongly have preferred for her to say nothing at all.

Thankfully, before tensions had a chance to rise, a loud voice called out from the marquee entrance.

"Tally Ho!" Melville said, a rather large bottle of Cognac in his right hand. "I found this little beauty in Father's cellar. You don't mind, do you father?"

Unsure what to say, Lord Montagu blushed slightly, cleared his throat, and then ignored his son's bluster in favor of continuing to converse with another guest about the dangers of the Treaty of Versailles.

"I thought as much!" Melville said as he strolled across the room to Eliza.

"And where have you been?" she asked, eyeing him suspiciously.

"Things to attend to, Old Girl," he grinned. "Thistlewood Estate won't run itself now, will it Cedric?"

"Do you really think a bottle of Cognac is a good idea, Mel?"

"Oh, come on," Melville beamed. "The night is young! Our dear sister is here with us. We have the esteemed Fairfaxes and Darlingtons for company, and, what's more, an old friend in our ranks! Isn't that right, Ollie, Old Bean?"

Ollie had been watching from the side, as he often did, but his eyes had rarely strayed from Eliza. He walked over and took the bottle of Cognac from Melville, studying the dust-covered label.

"My word, Mel. You really should ask your father's permission. This is an 1873 from the Hennesey private reserve."

Melville leaned into the group and whispered.

"Yes, but with company, Father won't want to appear stingy. Not in front of our esteemed guests, eh Jacob?"

"I'm game if you are, Old Chap," Jacob said as Melville waved one of the servers over and asked him to bring several brandy glasses.

"He never changes, does he?" Ollie said to Eliza, that charming smile once again dancing across his face.

"No, not really. And to think it's me the family is worried about."

Eliza was about to say something else when she found herself distracted by Lord Darlington, who had broken away from the group without saying a word and was heading towards the exit. Eliza found this action extremely peculiar. A man of aristocratic tendencies always excused himself from company when leaving, but in this case he had not. Eliza couldn't help but wonder if, perhaps, he was intimidated by the connection she clearly had with Ollie. After all, his move to the doorway had coincided with Ollie joining the group.

As he reached the doorway, he turned and locked eyes with Eliza, beckoning her with his hand before disappearing from view.

"I'd say he wants you to go after him," Ollie whispered.

"Would you want me to?"

"Well, that's not really up to me, Liza, now is it?"

"Always aloof, Ollie. For once I wish you'd say what you actually feel."

The clinking of glass broke the tension as Melville lifted several glasses from a server's tray and passed them around. Unsealing the old Cognac bottle, Melville pulled the cork, which answered with a pop. Gleefully, he began to add a small splash of brandy to everyone's glass.

"A shame my brother won't be here to taste this," Jacob said. "His lordship seems to have made a sharp exit. Perhaps he is hoping for another rendezvous, Miss Montagu?"

"Hardly."

"If you'd prefer a more enlightening chat by moonlight, I'd love to take a tour of the estate with you at some point."

"Quite popular tonight, aren't you, Eliza?" Ollie interjected.

"Maybe in a little while," Eliza said, hoping to see the slightest flicker of jealousy in Ollie's eyes.

"Make sure she takes you to the old swing," he said. "It's a special place for some privacy."

Before Eliza could think of a clever retort, the group was joined by Lady Montagu and Lady Darlington.

"Eliza, my dear, Lady Darlington and I were just discussing the tapestries in the old ball room. Why don't you free yourself from these men for a moment and accompany the good Lady."

"I'd be delighted, Lady Darlington." Eliza said, though that was not remotely true. "Please, this way."

Eliza guided Lady Darlington through the house and past the main staircase. It was only when they entered the East Wing that Lady Darlington began to talk.

"Ignore my boy, Jacob. He's a scamp. Always has been."

"I understand, believe me. We have one of them in Melville," Eliza said with a smile. "Jacob has his charms, though. I can't deny that. I wonder if you haven't set me up with the wrong son."

"You are not being set up with anyone, Miss Montagu," Lady Darlington said pointedly as they walked down a long hallway. "Surely you know this."

"Lord Darlington said—"

"Believe, me," the Lady continued, "I would rather my son marry up, not down, and though Thistlewood is a fine estate, it is downright pedestrian when compared to ours."

Once again, Eliza was cut off before she could say anything, this time by her father who suddenly marched in through the doorway from the main staircase.

"Your mother, Eliza. Really. Sending you off from the party like that. How can you get to know Lord Darlington if you aren't even in conversation with him?"

"He left abruptly, Father."

"Lord Montagu, I think we should concede that the association between my son and your daughter is not to be," Lady Darlington said.

"This is what happens when you treat our guests so poorly, Eliza!"

Eliza found herself caught off guard by how angry he appeared to be. She was even more caught off guard by just how much that hurt her.

"Father, let's not argue..."

"Argue? You—" He seemed flustered. "—You go and find Lord Darlington immediately, and you show him the sort of courtesy we Montagus are known for!"

"Father, I really..."

"Now!" This was unlike her father. He seemed vexed about the entire situation, but Eliza felt sure that there was something more at play. Something bubbling up underneath. So, she made the uncharacteristic decision to follow his wishes.

As she passed by the main staircase, Eliza spotted Frank flirting with a maid.

"Sorry to interrupt," she said, "but have you seen Lord Darlington?"

"Funny you should ask, Miss," Frank replied, obviously embarrassed at having been caught. "He asked me to give you this."

Frank passed over a note, which Eliza opened. It read:

Eliza, meet me in your room away from prying eyes and ears. There is something I need to tell you.
—Lord Darlington

It seemed odd to Eliza. Lord Darlington had mentioned having a drink after the dinner party, but something had clearly expedited things. And she was stunned that he had chosen her bedroom of all places. This was a serious breach of decorum.

Eliza moved swiftly up the central staircase and down to her bedroom. Although she did not want to be alone with Lord Darlington for long, she was curious enough about what he had to say that she had decided to entertain one drink before persuading him to rejoin the party downstairs.

She couldn't imagine whatever he had to say would be enough to convince her to marry him, but perhaps it would be enough to at least change her mind about him. He was forthright, she had to give him that. And after years of wondering what Oliver Fairfax was thinking, she found the idea of someone forthright appealing.

Plus, there was that comment he'd made about them both getting everything they wanted. What, exactly, did he think Eliza wanted? Was he arrogant enough to think just having him would be sufficient? Or had he heard about her mother's ultimatum? Was he open to some sort of arrangement that would still allow her to stay in London and paint?

As she turned the solid brass door handle to enter her bedroom, Eliza was surprised to find that she was almost excited to see him. Her mood promptly shifted, however, when she suddenly caught a scent that she couldn't quite identify. Though she did not recognize exactly what the smell was, she knew that it was similar to the chemical smell put off by some of her paints.

A cold dread washed over Eliza. Something was wrong; She felt it in her bones. She pushed the old oak door and was horrified to find the body of Lord Darlington lying in the center of the floor: his face pallid, his tongue bloated and protruding from his mouth, and the life gone forever from his eyes.

CHAPTER TEN

Eliza did not scream. She had never been one to panic, even in the worst of circumstances. Once, she saw a body in the canal, and rather than losing her head—and reinforcing all sorts of stereotypes as she did so—she had jumped in and fished the man out to check if he was breathing.

She'd hoped he was, of course, but it only took a moment to realize that he wasn't. She was sure that would be the case with Lord Darlington too. One only had to look at him to be certain of that. Still, Eliza hoped against hope that she was wrong, and she certainly wasn't going to alert anyone to the situation until she had exhausted all possibilities, no matter how improbable.

Eliza's hand trembled as she leaned over the body. Gently, she lifted Lord Darlington's wrist. She was surprised by the weight of his arm—so much heavier now that the life had gone out of it. She checked for a pulse and, finding none, grabbed a small hand mirror from her dresser. She held it up to his mouth, which she noted was surrounded by some sort of strange saliva residue. She desperately willed the mirror to fog, but it didn't.

There was no denying it. Lord Darlington was dead.

Still, while Eliza knew this to be true, she did not want it to be. She wanted someone to tell her that she was wrong. After all, she wasn't a doctor. Perhaps she'd made a mistake. Perhaps she'd simply failed to find his pulse and the mirror trick was the sort of thing that only worked in books.

Eliza rushed to the window of her room, opened it with some force, and then cried out to the marquee below:

"Is there a doctor down there?"

Quickly a mix of servants, guests, and family came out of the marquee, looking around to see where the scream had come from.

"Up here!" Eliza shouted down. "Lord Darlington has collapsed, and I can't find a pulse. Is there a doctor down there? Please, I need help!"

A cry then rose up to the window from the lawn. It was Lady Darlington. She was so distraught about Eliza's news that she fainted.

Luckily, she was caught in the sure hands of her other son, Jacob, otherwise they may have had two Darlingtons in need of a doctor.

"Stand back, stand back," Eliza's father said as he pushed through the shell-shocked crowd. "Parkins!" he shouted to the family butler. "Come!"

"Lord Darlington is up here in my room!" Eliza yelled. She knew that information would be scandalous—a belief that was only reinforced by the collective gasp that swept through the crowd, but Eliza knew there was no point in trying to hide it. Her father and Parkins needed to know where to go, and the news would find its way out eventually. The gossip mill was simply too strong to let something this big slip by unnoticed. No matter what Eliza did now, this would be the talk of the town for months, if not years, to come.

Lord Montagu and Parkins rushed up the stairs, a small crowd following behind them. A clatter of clambering feet and raised voices headed up the main staircase, and by the time Eliza opened the door to her room, she was faced with a mob-like crowd, both rushing to her aid and demanding answers.

Her father cut a more commanding figure than she expected. Indeed, he led the pack, his chest pushed out, marching quickly with the verve of a much younger man.

"Eliza, my dear!" He said loudly as he approached. "Step aside, please. Let us take care of this."

But as the crowd tried to press past her into the room, Eliza loudly told them to stop.

It seemed that she had inherited her commanding stance from her father's side.

"Is there a doctor or someone with a medical background?" she asked sternly.

"Parkins was a medic in the Boer war."

"But do we have a doctor?"

"No, Eliza. Now, out of the way. We need to get inside."

"Only you and Parkins, Father. Everyone else must stay out here."

"Why?" Jacob Darlington asked, his face etched in worry.

"Because," Eliza said as gently as she could, "I think he might have been murdered."

Jacob stood there dumbfounded as a stunned hush fell over the crowd.

Parkins, by this point, was already in the room, assessing Darlington. Lord Montagu assisted where he could. Eliza hoped beyond hope that her initial suspicions were untrue, that Lord Darlington had

had some sort of fit or turn, and that he would be all right—or, at the very least, that his death had been the result of natural causes.

Eliza, Jacob, and several others from the marquee waited anxiously outside the bedroom for news, but when Parkins emerged soberly from room, his head bowed, Eliza's heart sank. She knew, in this moment, that her instincts had been right.

"I'm terribly sorry, Sir," Parkins said, his attention directed at Jacob. "But it is true. Your brother has passed away."

Jacob stared on in disbelief, and, when it became clear that he might not be able to maintain his composure, Parkins, in a rare break of decorum, pulled the man close and allowed him to shield his tears from view on his shoulder.

Lord Montagu emerged from the room a moment later and held Jacob firmly around the arm.

"Steady, steady, Old Chap. Stiff upper lip and all that," he said in a calming voice.

"Mother...How will I tell her?" Jacob asked, his bottom lip quivering just slightly.

"We'll help, dear boy. We'll help," Lord Montagu assured him.

Lord Montagu placed his steady hand on Jacob's back, and together, the two began to make their way down the staircase, the unexpected mourners following slowly in their footsteps.

As they made their way back into the lobby, Eliza turned to Parkins.

"Was he...?"

Eliza's voice trailed off then. She couldn't bring herself to ask the question. To actually utter the word.

"I'm afraid so, m'lady," Parkins said. "It appears Lord Darlington was murdered."

***

Eliza sat in her father's study in stunned silence. Neither her mother nor her father said a word. In fact, the only noise at all was the sound of Lady Darlington sobbing into her son's arms.

"Not my son," she sobbed. "Not my son!"

"I know...I know..." Jacob whispered soothingly.

There was a great deal about Lady Darlington that Eliza found deeply objectionable, but in this moment, that didn't matter. Watching her grieve her son was excruciating, and Eliza's heart broke for her.

The sobbing was briefly interrupted by a knock the door.

"Who is it?" Lord Montagu asked.

"Parkins, your Lordship."

"You may enter."

"Sir," Parkins said as he opened the old, oak door and entered the room. "A Constable Salisbury has arrived downstairs. He is talking with Cedric at the moment, but he wishes to speak with Eliza next since she is the one who found the body."

"Of course," Lord Montagu said. "Assuming you feel up to it, Eliza."

Eliza was holding a large belt of single malt in her glass, but she had not touched it. Thoughts were rushing through her mind about Lord Darlington and the discovery of the body, and, if she was to be questioned by the police, she wanted to be as unclouded as possible.

"Why don't we both go?" Eliza asked, taking her father's hand.

Lord Montagu nodded, and the two stood and followed Parkins out of the study and down the main staircase. At the foot of the stairs stood a police constable in black uniform, his Bobby hat under his arm. He was talking to Cedric, which Eliza expected, but she found herself surprised that Melville was nowhere to be seen.

"Constable Salisbury," Parkins boomed as he reached the bottom of the stairs. "May I present Lord Montagu and one of the ladies of Thistlewood House, Miss Eliza Montagu."

"You can dispense with the airs and graces." Salisbury said, his face long and drawn. The brown mustache on his upper lip was small and well-groomed, but if the world could birth poor diplomacy in the flesh, it would be Constable Arthur Salisbury,

"Of course Constable," Lord Montagu said. "A man is dead."

"Yes, and I believe it was you who found him, Miss Montagu?"

"Yes," Eliza answered. "It was quite a shock. I found him..."

"You can give all salient information to Constable Phillips...Phillips!" Salisbury shouted.

A lanky, young officer with sandy-blond hair entered the lobby from a door on the right. He appeared to be eating a slice of chiffon cake with a delicate raspberry frosting, holding beneath it a white china plate. Somehow, he managed this fine balancing act while holding his police hat under one of his arms.

"I see talking to the kitchen staff is going well?" Salisbury said, rolling his eyes.

"Sorry, Sir," Phillips replied, his mouth still full of cake. "I was doing as you asked, taking a headcount of the staff, and the cook offered me some cake."

"Please, would you just…" Salisbury sighed. "This is Miss Eliza Montagu. She found the body. Would you take down the details while I look upstairs?"

"Yes, Sir…" Phillips said, wiping crumbs from his mouth. "Right away."

Phillips grinned at Eliza, and as he did, more crumbs fell to the floor.

Parkins then led Constable Salisbury upstairs to Eliza's room, while Eliza answered Phillips's questions. She laid out all the events in detail, but poor Philips seemed unable to keep up, scribbling frantically in his little black policeman's notebook while asking Eliza several times to repeat something or slow down.

Eliza empathized with the man, but she was starting to get frustrated. It had been an extraordinarily long evening, and the weight of the night's events were beginning to settle over her like a thick blanket. All she wanted to do was go to bed, but she had now been through her version of events three times, and Phillips seemed no closer to sorted than he had at the start.

It was then that Eliza heard footsteps on the main staircase. I

"Constable!" Lady Darlington's shrill voice struck down from above like ice. "I demand an update. I demand to know what happened to my son!"

Phillips cleared his throat.

"We're still making enquiries…"

"Not any longer," Constable Salisbury said, unexpectedly appearing on the scene, Parkins and Lord and Lady Montagu trailing along behind him. "Your suspicions were correct. Lord Darlington was murdered, and given the timeline of events, I believe he was killed by someone in this very house."

Constable Salisbury reached the floor of the lobby and then stood, surveying the group.

"Lord Montagu, I'm afraid I am going to have to ask you and all of your guests to remain here at Thistlewood House. No one is allowed to leave or enter the grounds until the inspector arrives."

"I refuse to stay in this house of murderers one more second!" Lady Darlington screamed. "Take me home this instant, Jacob!"

"Mother, Please…"

Eliza suspected Jacob wanted to plead with her further, but he did not appear to have the strength. He had suddenly turned a ghastly pale color, and Eliza instantly found herself worried that the same fate that befell his brother might befall him too.

"I say, Old Chap," Lord Montagu said. "You don't look too good...Parkins?"

Parkins gestured to a nearby servant, who promptly brought a chair over to Jacob and helped him sit down.

"Thank you," he said, patting his brow with a handkerchief

"Do you need a doctor, Sir?" Salisbury asked.

"No, just some water, please."

A glass of water was quickly poured for Jacob, who clutched it with shaking hands.

"I understand this is a difficult situation for everyone," Salisbury said loudly. "But justice must be done. Rest assured, when the inspector arrives, we will get to the bottom of this. In the meantime, I want each of you to give statements to Philips here. Miss Montagu, you'll need to come with me.

Eliza nodded and started to follow after him. As she did, Parkins grabbed her arm. Eliza turned to him, caught deeply off guard by the break in protocol.

"I'm sorry, m'lady," he whispered. "But you must be careful. I overheard the Constable speaking to Phillips and..."

"Spit it out, Old Chap. I'm in a bit of a hurry here."

"I don't know how to say this, m'lady, but...well, Constable Salisbury is determined to see someone hanged for this and, at the moment, you're the primary suspect."

CHAPTER ELEVEN

Salisbury sat at Lord Montagu's ornate writing desk in the study. He studied the room for a moment, his expression one part awe at the exquisite craftsmanship and rare books and two parts disdain for the ostentatious displays of wealth.

Eliza took a seat in one of the leather armchairs and watched him. She knew that look, and she began to worry that her family's lifestyle might prove a hindrance here—that he might be so blinded by his disgust at what they represented that he would not give any of them a fair shake.

"Constable Salisbury," she began, hoping that if she started the conversation, she could be the one to steer it. Unfortunately, Salisbury interrupted her before she was even able to finish the first sentence.

"Miss Montagu, when the Inspector arrives, he will make quick work of sorting out who is lying and who is telling the truth. So, it would behoove you to tell me the truth now."

"You think I would lie to you, Constable?"

"Everyone is capable of lying, Miss Montagu, and a whole lot worse. Theft, violence, and even murder, regardless of their title or status. If you think that your membership in this family—"

"I don't expect to be treated any differently, Constable," Eliza said, this time interrupting him before he'd had the chance to finish his sentence. "In fact, I would be angry if I were."

There was something in his assertion that riled Eliza. She was not some sort of elitist who thought that she deserved special treatment because of her class. She identified with those who thought Thistlewood and places like it were needlessly opulent, and it made her uncomfortable to be spoken to as though she were just some other entitled rich girl.

"I'm glad we're on the same page then," Salisbury said pointedly. "But know this: If I suspect you or any of your family members are lying about tonight's events, I will make it a point of pride to put the handcuffs on you myself. Understood?"

Eliza nodded.

"Good. Now, tell me, where and when did you find the deceased?"

"After dinner, at about nine PM. And you know full well he was in my room."

"Your room, indeed," he said, giving Eliza a pointed, judgmental look that she found utterly infuriating before scribbling in his black notebook. "And in what condition did you find the body?"

Eliza felt uncomfortable remembering the scene. She still hadn't processed the horror of the discovery, and she didn't appreciate being made to go through all this again.

"Lying on the floor on his stomach with his head turned slightly to the side. The air smelled lightly of chemicals."

At the mention of chemicals, Salisbury's eyes lit up.

"Chemicals, you say?" he said, continuing to scribble. "Describe them. Did they remind you of anything?"

Eliza's heart began to beat faster in her chest. There was something in his tone that made her feel as though she had been caught, even though she had not actually done anything. She wanted to tell Salisbury the truth, that the chemical smelled similar to an ingredient in her oil paints. Withholding that felt wrong. She wanted justice to be served, and she was afraid that she might be hindering that. But Parkins's words echoed loudly in her head. Salisbury was already suspicious of her. She could not afford to risk incriminating herself any further by showing knowledge of such things.

"No, Constable," she said, her tone calm despite the fact that having to lie in this moment turned her stomach. "It just smelled like a chemical. That's why I thought he was poisoned. That and some of the saliva residue on his mouth."

"A budding detective, are we?" Salisbury asked in a condescending tone.

"Wouldn't you want to find a killer if the murder had been committed in your home?"

"I heard you had quite the row with Darlington at dinner," Salisbury leaned forward on his chair, planted his elbows on the desk, and cupped his hands together. "Sounds like you might have had motive to me. And it is very convenient that you found the body. In my experience, that's as good a way to try to avoid suspicion as any."

Eliza wanted to storm out the room, but she knew that would only make things worse. If she flew off the handle, that would make it appear as though she didn't have control over her emotions. Normally, she kept her emotions in check because she didn't want to be seen as a "hysterical woman." Today, however, the stakes were higher. She didn't want to risk being seen as a killer.

"Lord Darlington and I did have a conflict at dinner. My family brought him here as a potential suitor, something I did not agree to, and I was summoned here under false pretenses. He was rude to the servants in a way that I found intolerable, and I did not want to be associated with that sort of behavior, nor did I want to be around it, so I walked out."

"And that was the last time you spoke with Darlington?"

"No. We spoke again when everyone transitioned to after-dinner drinks. It was far more civil, and there are at least a dozen witnesses who can testify to that effect. So, any theory you might have about me being angry enough about his attitude to kill him simply doesn't add up."

"And that was the only other time you spoke to him all evening?"

Eliza's mind flashed back to standing outside with Darlington on her way back to the stables. Lying to the Constable about that conversation felt risky, but telling the truth felt even riskier. The private drink they had arranged to have would have served as the perfect meet-up for an impromptu poisoning, and Eliza was afraid Salisbury would not believe her when she said it never actually occurred. That combined with the very public argument in the marquee, and she would look as guilty as sin.

So, while it pained her to withhold this information too, she decided that at this moment, it would be best not to tell the Constable about the conversation at all.

"Yes," Eliza said, her hands starting to sweat just slightly. "That was the only time I spoke with him."

"I see," Salisbury said, though there was something in his tone that made Eliza feel as though he did not entirely believe her—and that made her chest tighten in a way that made it almost hard to breathe.

"If it wasn't you, Miss Montagu, and let's be clear that at present I think it was, who do you think might have done it? Is there anyone else who would have had a reason to harm Lord Darlington or want him dead?"

Eliza sat in silence for a moment. She didn't want to imply that anyone was the murderer; however, she had a suspicion of her own, and it wouldn't do her case any harm if she shared it with the constable.

"You should speak with Barnsley," Eliza said finally. "Though, I suppose you'd have to find him first. I didn't see him in my room with the others or downstairs in the lobby. Don't you think it's curious that he didn't come to see what all the commotion was about?"

Salisbury wrote down the name, but Eliza wasn't convinced that he was taking her tip seriously, which she found incredibly frustrating. Barnsley was a good suspect—certainly better than her—and she was convinced that, if the constable could just take his blinders off for a moment, he would see that.

"Barnsley was the only person on the estate that I can think of who didn't have to answer to anyone tonight," she added, in an attempt to further make her case. "I, along with my family and our guests, were duty bound to attend the dinner party outside in the marquee. The servants are under constant supervision from our butler, the chef, and our head maid. Barnsley, on the other hand, had the run of the entire house tonight. I don't know what his motive would be, Constable, but he certainly had plenty of opportunity."

"Thank you, Miss Montagu," the Constable said. His expression was blank and his tone unchanged, so Eliza couldn't tell if any of what she said had landed. But she was glad to have said it anyway.

"Please let yourself out and tell Phillips I'd like to speak with each member of your family, as well as Lord and Lady Darlington."

"You'll want to speak with the Fairfaxes, too, I imagine."

"And they are?"

"Another family staying here tonight."

"Hm," Salisbury muttered as he jotted yet another note in his notebook.

"You will speak with Barnsley, won't you?" Eliza asked.

"Of course. We'll speak with everyone, Miss Montagu."

Salisbury returned his attention to his notebook, and Eliza got up to leave. As her hand reached for the doorknob, he interjected one last time.

"One more thing, Miss Montagu. I spoke with several members of the waitstaff downstairs before you came down. They suggested that you were gone for quite some time after you stormed out of the marquee. Perhaps even as long as forty-five minutes—leaving you more than enough time to have set up the murder. Can anyone vouch for your whereabouts during that period?"

Eliza turned around forcefully.

"Constable, you know very well that I was with Oliver Fairfax…"

"For a time," Salisbury interrupted. "But it seems as though he escorted your Great Aunt back to the marquee about twenty minutes into your strop around the grounds."

"Strop!? Listen here—"

"Which means I have not yet found anyone who can verify your whereabouts for the remainder of that time. Seems awfully suspicious, no?" Salisbury said with a smile. He was pleased with himself, and it made Eliza's blood boil.

"Perhaps you should be more diligent with your investigations before making baseless accusations, Constable Salisbury, "Eliza said, keeping her temper in check despite the rising heat in her cheeks. "I spoke with one of the stable hands for quite some time after Oliver left. I'm assuming it's not beyond your abilities to find this man and verify my account? He's probably still lying drunk in the hay."

Salisbury nodded, but the grin did not fade. He was enjoying putting Eliza under pressure.

"We'll see, Miss Montagu," he said. "The truth will come out in the end. Of that I can assure you."

Eliza left the room without bothering to reply. It was becoming increasingly clear that she could not trust the constable to properly investigate this murder. And there was far too much at stake for her to let that stand.

If this investigation is ever to arrive at the truth, she thought, *I may have to conduct it myself.*

***

"I'm sure all of this will get straightened out," Ollie said to Eliza gently.

"I hope so."

Just then, Salisbury descended the main staircase, stopping several stairs up to survey the guests and staff still assembled in the lobby. For a moment, no one spoke.

"I wish to leave!" Lady Darlington demanded suddenly.

"I'm afraid I can't let you do that, Lady Darlington," Salisbury replied. "Not until the Inspector has spoken with each of you and had a chance to review the scene of the crime."

"And when exactly will that be?" Lord Montagu asked. Eliza was a bit taken aback by his tone, but she understood it. This was a high-stress situation, and Salisbury's attitude was making everything worse.

"Not until morning."

"Morning!" Lady Darlington exclaimed. "This is outrageous!"

"Please, mother…"

"You can shriek all you like, Lady Darlington," Salisbury continued. "But I assure you, he is coming as quickly as possible. He is attending to another matter at present and will be here as soon as that is done."

"Another matter that involves the murder of a Lord!?" Lady Darlington asked, her voice now a mixture of quivering rage and outright shock.

"Lords in their castles and the rest of us peasants are all the same in the eyes of the law, Lady Darlington. You'd all best remember that."

"Listen here—" Lady Darlington began, but Salisbury was having none of it.

"I suggest you go get some rest," he continued, in a tone that made it quite clear this was anything but a suggestion. "Tomorrow is going to be quite intensive. And before any of you get any ideas and decide to start playing amateur detective, please know that Phillips and I will be standing guard all evening. We expect you to stay in your rooms, and failure to do so will bring significant consequences."

Eliza knew better than to argue. So, it seemed, did everyone else. The crowd quickly began to disperse, with servants and aristocrats alike wandering off to their respective rooms—all except Eliza, whose room was now a crime scene.

"Are you okay, Eliza?" Ollie asked in a hushed voice.

It had been a long day, and much as she hated to admit it, there was nothing she wanted more than to rest in the comfort and reassurance of Ollie's warm embrace. But she was not about to give him the satisfaction of seeing her vulnerable. Not after the way he'd behaved. So, instead, she simply said: "I am...Good night, Oliver," before walking out of the lobby and heading down to the room where she'd left the dog earlier that evening.

"Hello, Boy," Eliza said soothingly, as the dog ran up to greet her. "Looks like we're keeping each other company for the night."

Eliza got undressed and climbed in between the sheets of the four-poster bed. The dog looked up at her, pleadingly.

"Oh, all right. Up you come."

The dog leapt onto the bed and nestled in beside her. In a matter of minutes, he was fast asleep, and Eliza marveled at how an animal could go through so much only to forget it in an instant. In some ways, she longed to be just like that—to be able to forget all of the trauma she had witnessed this evening. But she could not afford to. Constable Salisbury had it in for her and her family, and if she did not find a way to get to the truth, she or someone she loved could wind up hanged for a crime they did not commit.

CHAPTER TWELVE

Eliza awoke the next morning with a gasp, her heart furiously pounding as the result of a vicious nightmare about Lord Darlington's death. Her nightgown clung to her, and her hair was drenched with sweat. Eliza practically drunk in the morning sun that was peeking through her window, desperate to reassure herself that it was morning and it had all been nothing but a bad dream.

The problem was that that was only half true. Lord Darlington was still dead, and she was still a prime suspect. If justice was going to be done, Eliza had work to do.

Eliza rushed through her morning routine and started down the hallway, her new canine companion trotting eagerly alongside her. The corridors were still quiet around her, but the smell of their head chef Rene's delicious breakfast concoctions wafted through the house and reached her all the way in the West Wing. The smell of bacon hit her first, followed by something sweeter. A pastry perhaps—like a crumpet or a scone. Eliza couldn't say for sure just yet, but whatever it was, Eliza was eager to find out and devour it, and she knew the dog would be too. That's why she was so surprised when he suddenly stopped and started walking in the other direction.

"Come back here!" Eliza cried, but the dog did not heed her. Instead, he scampered further away in the wrong direction, moving from corridor to corridor before finally stopping and standing next to a closed door.

"There you are," she said softly. "Come here, little fellow."

As Eliza reached the dog and patted it on the head, she noticed the sound of voices nearby. Usually, Eliza would have been courteous and given them their privacy, but these were far from usual circumstances. Plus, unless she had misunderstood, whoever was in there had just said her name.

Eliza stepped forward quietly and rested her ear against the cold, wooden door. It took only a moment for her to realize that the voices belonged to Lady Darlington and Jacob, and they appeared to be having a fight.

"Mother, calm down," Eliza heard Jacob say. The frustration in his voice was apparent, and Eliza felt sorry for him. She could only imagine what a trying time this must have been.

"This will not stand, Jacob," Lady Darlington insisted. "That Eliza Montagu is a bad seed. She murdered your poor brother because she's some kind of conchy. She hates people like us. Hates us! I won't stay here another minute. I've already lost one child to that witch, and I'll not lose another."

"Mother, please," Jacob sighed. "You can't seriously think I'm in danger?"

"And why not?" scoffed Lady Darlington. "I came here at the behest of your brother, Jacob. I should never have listened to him and allowed this sordid meeting in the first place. I mean, a Montagu and a Darlington married!? Preposterous! And now because we're not behind the idea, they're finishing us off!"

"Mother, that's a ridiculous notion," Jacob said, this time more firmly. "I agree; we must get to the bottom of this, but to do that, we have to stay put. At least for now."

"I will not spend another night under the same roof as that family!" Lady Darlington said, her voice suddenly raised.

"People will hear you, Mother."

"Let them!" she shouted before switching tact. "Please, my son, take me away from here. Please..." she said, her voice suddenly soft and desperate.

"Perhaps the Constable will allow us to stay in one of the smaller guest properties on the estate. That way, we're not sleeping under the same roof as Charlie's killer, whoever that may be, but also won't look like we're running away either. To do so would look suspicious. And you, more than anyone know the importance of keeping up appearances."

Lady Darlington could not argue with that. For a moment, all was silent, and then, suddenly, Eliza heard a footfall on the other side of the door. Thanks to the creaking floorboards, it was apparent that someone was moving towards her.

Swiftly, Eliza darted up the corridor and around the corner out of view, but, as soon as she felt safe, she realized that the dog had not followed her. Instead, he had stayed put and was still standing directly outside the door. Eliza winced as she heard the subtle creak of a door opening followed by a startled voice.

"Oh! Hello, little fellow," Jacob said.

Lady Darlington poked her head out to see who Jacob was talking to and, upon realizing it was a dog, looked down with absolute disgust. "Horrible little thing…Just like the Montagus to let him roam free through the halls like this. Doing its business wherever it pleases, no doubt. These people—"

"He looks like a bloodhound," Jacob interrupted. "He probably came from one of the stables. I should take him round there and see if he escaped. With all the cooking going on, he probably snuck in in search of a snack. Come here, young chap."

Eliza could not bear the thought of the dog going back to the stables, so she did the only thing she could.

"Oh, there you are, Darling," she said as she marched over towards the dog. She smiled cordially at the Darlingtons, which required no shortage of effort in light of the accusations Lady Darlington had just been making.

"Is this…thing yours, then?" Lady Darlington asked.

"Yes, he is. Thank you for finding him, I was worried sick."

"Miss Montagu, I—"

"Look here, Montagu," Lady Darlington said before her son had even begun to finish his thought. "We want nothing to do with you or your dog. If it were up to me, I would march you out of here right now and take you straight to the gallows."

"Lady Darlington," Eliza said with a sigh. "Believe what you like, but I had nothing to do with the death of your son."

"My Mother doesn't—"

"I can speak for myself, Jacob!" Lady Darlington interrupted once more, pushing past Eliza and out into the hallway. "If you cannot even support your mother in her hour of need, what use are you anyway!" Lady Darlington all but screamed before storming down the hallway.

Jacob, however, just stood there.

"Aren't you going to go after her?" Eliza asked.

Jacob shook his head. Eliza felt for him. The poor man looked exhausted and utterly defeated.

"I'd ask how you are, but…" Eliza trailed off. She wasn't quite sure what to say, but she felt as though she should say something.

"I'll be fine," Jacob said, rubbing his forehead. "It's just…There's an expectation of me now, and it's ruined everything."

Eliza knew immediately what he was referring to. It was a feeling she'd had herself countless times.

"I'm not cut out for any of this," he continued. "And being stuck in this house is not helping one jot. No offense."

"None taken. I love this house, but I know better than anyone how being stuck here can start to feel like a prison."

Suddenly, Eliza had an idea.

"Come with me. I think I know something that might help. It's not quite as good as a vacation, but with a little creative thinking, it can feel like an escape."

Eliza led Jacob and the dog back down the hallway and over to the glass conservatory where she had encountered Barnsley the previous night. Eliza could see a weight lift off of him as he looked about at the exotic plants and trees before him. The sun gleaming in through the glass surroundings was a tonic, and Eliza was grateful to have been given the chance to provide it.

The dog mulled around, smelling the musty soil and disappearing here and there into bushes of overgrown plants.

"He seems like a keen one. What's his name?"

Eliza was struck by the fact that she hadn't even thought about that yet. Certainly, there had been a great deal going on, but still, the animal deserved a name. She decided to go with the first one that came to mind.

"Scout,"

"Well, he's doing a good job of it," Jacob said with a laugh.

"I am sorry about your brother, Jacob," Eliza said softly as the two wandered along the paths of the greenhouse. "I had no ill will towards him."

"I know...My mother is just desperate to find his killer, and you...You do fit the bill in some ways."

Eliza wanted to say something, to defend herself, but to do so felt insensitive in light of his obvious grief. So instead, in a rare moment of deference, she simply let him talk.

"It's not that I think you poisoned my brother, Eliza," he continued. "But you must look out for yourself because there's no doubt that Salisbury fellow sees you as a suspect."

"I know. That became very apparent in my chat with him last night...I've been wracking my brain for an alternate suspect, but I just can't figure out who in this house would want your brother dead."

"I've been asking myself that same question. My brother could be a bore, and he took all his responsibilities as head of the family far too seriously, but he was a good man deep down."

"He's known for his business dealings, is he not?" Eliza asked. "I remember reading about him in the broadsheets a few years ago. He secured several large estates as part of a business takeover. I believe one was an ancestral home of a competitor…William something…"

"Renault?"

"Yes! That was the one. Wouldn't someone like that have an eye for revenge when it comes to your brother?"

"Possibly someone like him, but definitely not him specifically. William Renault died of malaria a few months ago on a trip to Africa."

"Someone else, then?" Eliza thought out loud.

"My brother has ruffled more than a few feathers, but murder?"

"I know the police will probably ask you this, but, if you think of any enemies he might have had, would you perhaps write down their names and give them to me?"

Jacob looked at Eliza with an expression that was a blend of curiosity and respect.

"I'm sure the police can—"

"Salisbury already has it in for me and my family. He'd love nothing more than to find out one of those 'toffs in their mansion' is guilty of murder so he can cart them away. If you'll trust me, I'd like to do some detective work of my own and help find your brother's killer."

"How could I ever decline a lady?" he said with a smile before walking past Eliza and heading towards a large plant with an unusual flower. The flower itself had a pink hue to it and was several inches across. A bobbled circle of white and green was at its center, and it hung on a stem that was vast, almost two meters in height.

"This isn't a King Protea, is it?"

"You know your flowers," Eliza said as she walked over to Jacob.

"Not really," he said, sheepishly. "Just a few. There's a girl who is fond of these."

Jacob blushed a bit then, and Eliza couldn't help but smile.

"Now, this is a very different Jacob to the one I saw at the dinner party. A girl you have your eye on, no doubt?"

"Yes. In South Africa, where these flowers come from. I was looking forward to heading there later in the year, but…"

"Your brother?"

Jacob nodded solemnly.

"He always looked after Mother and the family business, and I was grateful for that. Truth be told, I've always found responsibility to be a prison. With Charlie gone, now it's one from which I shall never escape."

Eliza pitied Jacob. She knew all too well the prisons that Society could forge. They were wrought from expectation with bars made, not of iron, but of tradition and duty. And the prison warden, well, in Eliza's life at least, the warden took on an uncanny resemblance to that of her own mother. She suspected that was the case for Jacob as well, a suspicion that was only confirmed by what he said next.

"Thank you so much for the chat, Eliza, but I'm afraid I must be getting back to Mother."

Eliza gently patted Jacob on the shoulder on his way out before going off in search of Scout. As she scoured the conservancy in search of him, she thought more about what Jacob had said. She felt her pulse quicken at the reminder that, while Jacob's prison might be strictly metaphorical, if she did not get to the bottom of this mystery soon, the prison she could find herself in would be very, very real.

CHAPTER THIRTEEN

Scout sat underneath the table by Eliza's legs, his face occasionally irritated by the movement of the drooping tablecloth. The room was bright and breezy, and beyond the open windows, the green of the estate beckoned. But Eliza could not walk out there and lose herself in the lush woods the way she had as a child, and neither could her family. Instead, they sat together around a large oak table covered in white linen and ate breakfast. They were trying to pretend that things were normal, but Eliza knew that they were not. And with each passing hour, she grew more and more afraid that they never would be again.

They ate in the family's private breakfast chamber. The room was rarely used, as the family normally had breakfast alongside guests, but not this morning. For Eliza, this was a relief. Lady Darlington's accusations appeared to be making the rounds, and they seemed to have been enough to turn the tide of opinion against her. Eliza had passed several servants on the way to the breakfast room, and the way they avoided her gaze was telling. The rumors were spreading fast.

Eliza the murderer.

No one had said much at the table so far. Eliza was eating a delicate, homemade croissant with rich, blackberry jam. Rene had made it from blackberries he'd plucked from the estate, and you could taste the difference. Eliza had never been able to find its equal—even in the whole of London.

As Eliza slipped a small piece of the rich, buttery pastry to Scout, the others tucked into a full English breakfast complete with eggs, bacon, and black pudding. Black pudding was something Eliza could never entirely stomach. Although she had not become a vegetarian yet, the idea of eating another animal's blood reminded her of something out of a Bram Stoker novel.

Mercy was the first to break the silence.

"It's so good to have you here with us, Liza," she said with a smile.

"It's lovely to be here," Eliza replied, though she only half meant it. She was delighted to see her family, but given the arranged courtship her family had sprung on her and the murder of Lord Darlington, she could hardly be blamed for wishing the reunion had come under more palatable circumstances.

"Perhaps, when all of this blows over, we could all go for a nice picnic in the country," Mercy suggested.

"There's been a murder," Great Aunt Martha said, her face the picture of exasperation, "and all this one can think about is frolicking around in the glade. This is precisely what's wrong with the current generation."

While Eliza understood Great Aunt Martha's point about the seriousness of the moment, she couldn't stand to see Mercy being chided like that.

"I think it's a perfectly splendid idea, Mercy," Eliza said, hoping to take the sting out of Great Aunt Martha's comment. "Perhaps I can get my paints down, and we can do a family portrait. It certainly would be nicer than the harsh faces on the walls of the staircase."

"They always make me think of an old ghost story," Mercy added. "I don't know why we keep them around."

Lady Montagu squirmed in her seat. "It is a great honor to be the current owners of Thistlewood House, Mercy. We are part of a long line of owners who have helped shape this country into what it is today. The least we can do is honor their memory as we hope to be honored in the future."

Lord Montagu grumbled something under his breath that Eliza could not make out.

"Oh, come now, spit it out, Father," Eliza said.

Cedric, sitting at the end of the table, immaculately dressed despite the fact that it was only family breakfast, hid his smile underneath his hand in response.

"Your father has a lot on his mind, Eliza," Lady Montagu said sharply.

"Everything is ruined..." Lord Montagu said. "The business deal with the Darlingtons and the Fairfaxes is off."

"Business deal?" Eliza said, astonished that this was the place her father had chosen to place his focus, in light of everything that had happened. "A man is dead, father. That certainly warrants more grief than a business deal."

"And what do you know about business?" Great Aunt Martha snapped. "You live off your father's money, and you've never made so much as a dollar.

Eliza's face flushed at that. Her Great Aunt Martha always did have a way of going precisely for the jugular.

Lord Montagu sighed. "No, Eliza is correct. We must put these things into perspective."

"Where's Melville?" Eliza asked quietly.

"Probably in a bush somewhere with an empty bottle of Cognac."

"Cedric! Enough of that," Lady Montagu chastised. "You know your brother is a fragile sort. He's probably overwhelmed by the murder."

"Overwhelmed by gin," Cedric said drily.

This time, it was Eliza's turn to laugh.

"Oh, my head," Melville said, walking in through the open doorway as though summoned by the words of his family, looking disheveled and still wearing the same clothes from the previous night.

"Sit over here." Eliza patted the chair to her right. "If you think you can make it."

"I'm fine, I'm fine," Melville said as he made his way towards the chair and sat down a little lopsided. His hair was ruffled, and it was clear that the bright sunshine was causing him discomfort.

"Now," said Cedric, grinning towards his brother. "How about a nice fried duck egg for breakfast?"

"You swine," Melville growled under his breath, nearly turning green in response.

"We will not have that sort of language at the table," Great Aunt Martha said, tapping the tabletop with her fist. She was certainly stronger than both her looks and age inclined anyone to believe.

The cutlery made a rattling sound in response, and Melville winced at the thump.

There was another quiet period as Melville was served some toast and water, something his stomach would have found much more agreeable, and the conversation soon turned to what would happen next.

"Father, when will the Inspector arrive?" Eliza asked.

"I should expect soon," he said gravely. "I've heard a bit about him. Younger chap. Tenacious. He's investigated a number of serious crimes in London over the last few years. I have no idea why he has ended up here, but he has."

The room fell tensely quiet. In an effort to break the tension Lord Montagu turned to Eliza and smiled.

"A good thing he only got going after you had left Thistlewood, my dear. Think of what he would have made of your hijinks."

Eliza smiled, but it didn't quite reach her eyes. She simply could not be jovial this morning. Not when their lives were on the line.

Melville, noting the change in his sister, leaned back in his chair and patted her on the back affectionately.

"Jokes aside," Lord Montagu said, "I need you all to be at your most wary. This Constable Salisbury chap has it in for us, and if the Inspector is similar at all, any one of us could be in danger. The important thing is to be honest while trying to limit the scandal of this situation as much as possible. If we get out of this with the Montagu name unscathed, we will be doing well."

Eliza thought about her conversation with Salisbury and how she had omitted her meeting with Lord Darlington at the front of the house. Indeed, she had kept the details of her planned drink with the man secret from everyone. And now, the poor fellow was dead. She had to find out who the killer was before the finger was pointed even more firmly at her.

"I hope they speak with Barnsley," Eliza said.

Lord Montagu looked drawn for a moment. His breathing became deeper.

"Be careful, Eliza," Great Aunt Martha said sharply. "Barnsley is very…dear to this family."

"Is he, now? Then why have I never heard of him before?"

Lord Montagu cleared his throat. "My dear, he is an old friend who is recuperating here. He is best left to his own business. The man would not hurt a fly, and I do not want such thoughts put into the heads of Salisbury and the Inspector, do you understand?"

"It might be a little too late for that, Father. I mentioned him to Constable Salisbury during our talk yesterday."

A grave change came over Lord Montagu. His usual affable way melted, and he stood up from the table, wiping his mouth with a napkin and discarding it on the table in front of him.

"Barnsley will be left out of this! We do not need the police poking their noses in our affairs, nor those of our friends. Leave the man alone!"

"Surely it's best that someone outside of the family is seen as a suspect rather than one of us?" Eliza said, utterly baffled by her father's reaction.

"Barnsley is not a suspect!" Lord Montagu said. It was clear he was trying to regain his composure, but it was obviously a struggle. "Barnsley is a close friend, Eliza. He must be left alone and to his own devices. Now, if you'll excuse me, I have some matters to attend to."

Lady Montagu and Great Aunt Martha followed, both stopping to once more glare at Eliza on their way out the door. Their disapproval didn't bother her. She was used to that. She was not, however, used to her father being so abrupt with her. Much as she hated to admit it, that stung.

"I'm sorry, Father," she said. "I didn't mean to upset you."

"It's not your fault, Eliza," he said, though he did not look her in the eye. "I should not have raised my voice. Just…Please do as I ask."

With that Lord Montagu left, leaving Eliza alone with her siblings.

"What was all that about?" she asked, once she was sure they were out of earshot.

"I don't know," Mercy said. "I don't like that Barnsley, though. I've seen him around the house, and there's something…strange about the way he looks at it."

"Oh, Mercy," Cedric said. "You're always living a fantasy. Barnsley is no more interested in this house than he is in conversation. He just wants to be left alone."

"Have you spoken with him before?"

Cedric pulled out his pipe and began to press tobacco into it from a pouch in his breast pocket.

"I've tried to approach the man on a number of subjects. He's always civil more or less, but there's always an excuse to leave before I can find out anything about him. I think Father is correct, the man has clearly suffered some severe psychological wound from the war."

"Do you think he's wounded enough to kill Lord Darlington?" Melville asked. Clearly, the hangover made him blunter than anyone else in the room.

"There are plenty of poor chaps with shell shock who never became violent," Eliza said. "But…"

"But what?" Mercy asked enthusiastically.

"Does anyone think Father is keeping something from us?"

Melville said something about their father always having a lot on his mind, but the words were indistinct to Eliza; the worry was not. There was something bothering Father even before the murder. Something was going on. Something terrible. She could feel it in her bones.

CHAPTER FOURTEEN

After breakfast, Eliza headed out for a walk in the conservatory to clear her head. Scout followed in tow, gleefully wagging his tail and looking at his new human friend with increasing devotion.

As Scout dashed through a row of tulips, Eliza tried to sort out her thoughts. There were two things that were troubling her this morning: either of them in isolation would have been enough to cause worry, but together they might, in the wrong hands, cause suspicion.

The first was that her family had invited the Darlingtons to their home. Eliza was certain that Constable Salisbury would think this could have been a cover. No one in their right mind would think that a family would invite someone to their home to murder them, and that was why it might be seen as too convenient—the perfect plan to avoid suspicion.

The second worry was the way that Eliza's father had responded to her inquiries about the mysterious Barnsley. She had rarely known her father to hide anything from her or her siblings, but she had a growing unease in the pit of her stomach that told her this was exactly what was happening.

Eliza found it difficult to reconcile Darlington's murder and her father's secrecy. If she thought it looked suspicious, Salisbury would be on that fact like a man served his last meal. She could not figure out why her father seemed so determined to protect this man—this man that neither she, nor her siblings, had ever heard of prior to his arrival.

She needed more information on him, but she wasn't sure where to find it. Her father was a stone. If he didn't want to share the information, there would be no cracking him. What she needed was someone he would have trusted enough to confide in, someone who knew his secrets. More than that, she needed someone who also trusted her enough to share them, which certainly ruled out her mother.

And that's when it hit her. Parkins!

Swiftly, and with Scout at her side, Eliza set off in search of the old seadog. She checked at least half a dozen places inside Thistlewood house before finally spotting him in the servant's quarters, providing a strict overview of the marching orders for the day.

Just like Parkins, Eliza thought. *Not even a murder could convince him to let a piece of silverware go unpolished or a tablecloth left askew.*

After he dismissed the servants, Parkins turned and spotted Eliza.

"Miss Montagu!" he said, surprised. "What are you doing here?"

"I've come to see you," Eliza said with a smile.

"And who is this little chap?" Parkins asked, bending at the knees to reach the dog for a good scratch behind its ears.

"I've named him Scout. One of the damned stable hands was giving him a bad time, so I've taken him in."

"Would you like me to reprimand him, Miss?" said Parkins. Whenever he stood up, he instinctively held the rigid, proud stance of a man who had spent years in the military.

"That's alright, Parkins. I have a feeling that the fellow was having a bad time as it is."

"Always the compassionate one" Parkins said, a slight flicker of pride in his eye. "It is an honor to see the noble Lady you have become."

Eliza blushed at the compliment. Parkins's opinion mattered far more to her than most of the people on the estate, including many of the members of her own family, and she was honored to have his approval.

"Thank you, Parkins. That means a great deal."

"Simply speaking the truth, Miss."

Eliza beamed at him before shifting conversational gears.

"Parkins, what do you make of this Barnsley fellow?"

"Ah, yes, your father's guest…"

Eliza could swear she heard a hint of disapproval in Parkins's tone, which was completely out of character for him. She was becoming more and more convinced that Parkins was the right person to talk to by the second.

"Do you think he could have killed Lord Darlington?" Eliza asked.

"I would never wish to lay murder at the feet of any guest here at Thistlewood House, Miss. However, murder has indeed been committed. As for Mr. Barnsley, while I do not know of his intentions here, I cannot say that he is any more likely a murderer than anyone else."

"Oh, come on, Parkins. Level with me. What's this Barnsley fellow up to?"

"That is between your father and Mr. Barnsley, Miss. I have not been privy to those conversations."

"You and your etiquette, Parkins." Eliza said with a sigh. And then, she was hit with a memory from her childhood—a way in which, as a girl, Eliza had managed to get information out of Parkins that he would not have otherwise shared. A way that might just get her what she needed now.

"Okay, Parkins. I tell you what: Say nothing if you think Barnsley is a danger to my family."

For a moment, Parkins appeared flustered, his cheeks growing red. Crucially, however, he indeed said nothing.

"Loyal to the end, old friend," Eliza said with a smile. "You know something, but you don't want to break my father's confidence."

"As I say, Miss, I have not been officially privy to those conversations."

Parkins's statement sparked another line of inquiry in Eliza's mind. *Of course,* she thought. *The servants! They likely know more than anybody!*

"Parkins, do you think any of the servants saw or heard anything last night?"

"I have considered it. But I have not had the time to speak with all of the staff individually, as of yet, so I cannot say for sure. If I do find out something, do you—"

"Yes, please, Parkins. Let me know anything you find out. And also…"

"Is everything all right, Miss?"

Something had occurred to Eliza, but she wasn't sure how to share it with Parkins. She knew he would be upset, and she hated upsetting him. But she also didn't like the idea of lying to him either. So, she decided to go with the truth gently shared.

"Parkins…The servants have access to most of the house, do they not?"

"Yes, Miss."

"And Lord Darlington was awful towards several of them during dinner…"

"I hope you are not insinuating what I think you are, Miss."

Eliza stepped forward and lowered her voice. "It's not beyond the realm of possibility, is it? After all, the servants were preparing and serving all of the food and champagne. They would have been perfectly situated to slip Lord Darlington the poison."

Finally, Parkins's military stance seemed to deflate slightly. He did not reply. He merely sighed for a moment as a worried expression spread across his face.

"If you do think of anything, Parkins. A member of staff who seemed particularly angered by the Darlingtons or a servant that disappeared out of view leading up to the murder, you will tell me, won't you?"

"For you, Miss, anything. However, the servants are my responsibility. I see many of them as my own family. The thought that they…"

Parkins stopped for a moment. Eliza could tell he was gathering himself, which caught Eliza off guard. Parkins had never been one for emotion, regardless of the circumstance.

"Motive is key, Miss," Parkins said, returning to the strong, formal cadence Eliza knew so well. "Why would a servant do such a thing? Because they were angered by a few badly spoken sentiments about Class?"

"Yes, that is the difficulty…Perhaps one of them cracked, or they had some other dealings with the man we've yet to uncover. Do you know if any of the servants previously worked for the Darlingtons?"

"Not that I am aware, but…"

"But what?"

"Recently, Lord Montagu let a considerable portion of the servants go…"

"He fired them?" Eliza asked.

Eliza was stunned by this revelation. When she first arrived at Thistlewood House, she had noticed there had been considerable changes to the staff since she'd left, but she'd been gone three years. While many of the servants in the higher-paid positions had been with her family for decades, it wasn't uncommon for there to be turnover in the lower-level positions. The female servants often left when they married, and the men frequently took higher-level positions in other houses.

Eliza had assumed everyone who left had done so voluntarily. The decision to let people go was most certainly out of character for her father. If anything, he was always guilty of hiring more people than were needed to run the estate.

"More like he replaced them. A few months ago, your father asked me to let go any staff members who could be deemed expendable or were more trouble than they were worth. This state of affairs persisted for a month or so, and then, suddenly he asked me to hire new staff to fill all of those positions. So, you see, Miss, there are at least twenty or so people on the estate who are new to Thistlewood House, and I could not with great confidence vouch for their histories or their characters beyond their references."

"Any ideas why this went on, Parkins?"

"No, Miss. My point, however, is that I cannot personally vouch for all the staff, and that Mr. Barnsley is not the only unknown quantity living and working at Thistlewood."

"Thank you, Parkins," Eliza said. "You've given me a lot to consider."

"I'm glad you came down," Parkins added. "You've saved me a trip. The Inspector is here, and I've been tasked with ensuring you speak with him today. Preferably sooner than later."

"I will do that shortly, Parkins," Eliza promised, as she moved past him and headed toward the door. Scout followed, wagging his tail. "But right now, there's someone else I need to speak to in order to get to the bottom of this."

"Might I advise that you be careful, Miss?"

"Careful?"

"There has already been one murder at Thistlewood. And in my experience, once someone has committed a murder, they can easily be moved to kill again. This house is not safe until the killer is found, and if you're not careful, I'm afraid you may find yourself in his way."

"Thank you, Parkins," Eliza replied. "Though I am a believer in equality, old friend. Who is to say that the killer isn't a woman?"

Parkins chuckled slightly, though Eliza could sense that he was genuinely on edge. She'd rarely seen Parkins afraid before, and it was jarring. She was starting to worry that he was right. Maybe she wasn't safe now—and the thought of not being safe in her childhood home chilled Eliza to her core.

She wasn't about to take his advice to be careful, though. If Parkins was right, Eliza didn't just need to catch the killer to save someone from being wrongfully convicted of murder. She needed to catch the killer before they had the chance to kill again.

CHAPTER FIFTEEN

If Eliza was right and one of the servants was the murderer, it stood to reason that they likely worked in the kitchen. After all, no one had easier access to Lord Darlington's food and drink than the kitchen staff—and no one knew the kitchen staff better than Rene.

Rene was one of the greatest chefs in all of Paris, so getting him to come here and work as the family's private chef had been a tremendous coup. Eliza's mother had bragged about it for months, and every one of her father's business associates had invented some excuse or another to come visit Thistlewood in a thinly veiled attempt to taste some of Rene's famous cooking.

The kitchen had always been one of Eliza favorite places at Thistlewood, even more so after Rene was hired, and she couldn't help but smile as she entered it. Parkins's words still haunted her, but she couldn't help being more relaxed here, surrounded by the smell of house-baked pastries and freshly brewed tea.

"Rene?" Eliza said as she entered the kitchen and surveyed the room. "Where the devil are you, Old Chap?"

"Mademoiselle Montagu!" came the delighted response—though Eliza could not see from where. There was a clatter of something hitting off metal, and then "Ah...My head!"

Eliza moved between two long, shiny, metal worktops before turning to the right by a wall lined with an array of cooking utensils. She let out a laugh as soon as she saw the source of the voice. Rene's lanky legs and bottom half were sticking out of a huge, cast-iron cooking oven.

"Come here, you silly oaf," Eliza said with a laugh, leaning over and helping pull him out from under the oven.

As he stood up, his slender figure towered over Eliza. Rubbing his head, he looked down at her with a frown that quickly melted away to an expression only encountered when meeting an old friend.

"Look at you, My Dear!" Rene said, surveying Eliza before taking her hand in his own and kissing the back of it.

"It's lovely to see you, Rene."

"And you, my dear. This old house hasn't been the same since you left. I heard a rumor you had returned but did not dare to believe it."

Eliza grinned. The last twenty-four hours had been a whirlwind, and she was grateful for the respite his easy company provided.

"Still stuck with that old wood stove, I see," Eliza said, pointing at the place where Rene had been half submerged.

"It's the only thing your father will not get rid of! I have tried telling him time and time again, we have gas, we can have a proper modern cooker, but he simply won't hear of it."

"You know, Dad. I love him, but he has always been a bit stuck in the past."

"Madame, we all have our fondness for what went before, but sometimes progress is a good thing! But look who I'm telling that to. Young Mercy often tells me about your adventures as a suffragette. Still fighting the good fight?"

"Always, Rene." Eliza said with a smile. She could tell Rene was proud of her, and that meant the world to Eliza. After all, his stories of travelling Vienna, Italy, and Belgium were part of what inspired her to leave Thistlewood in the first place.

"Have you eaten?" Rene asked. "I was about to begin preparing lunch. If you care to join me, I could offer you the first taste."

"Thank you, but I'm afraid I can't stay."

"Ah, you're a woman on a mission. I should have known."

"I would have come to visit you eventually, I promise. I really have been eager to see you. Things have just been very…full on."

"Yes, of course," Rene said. "I completely understand. Terrible shame about Lord Darlington."

"Agreed."

"I'm glad you stopped by," Rene said, as he reached for a batch of carrots from the garden and began going at them with a peeler. "There's something I must tell you."

"Is everything alright?" Eliza asked, concerned. There was something in Rene's tone that scared her, and she wasn't sure that she could handle any more bad news just then.

Rene sighed. "Yes, I suppose so. It's just, truth be told, I'm leaving Thistlewood. I've enjoyed my time here, but it's been five years and I think it is time to move on. I was never meant to stay in one place for such a long time."

"I understand. And I am certainly the last person who has any right to give anyone grief about leaving Thistlewood. But we will miss you terribly. Father, especially."

"Your father already knows. Last night's meal with the Darlingtons was supposed to be my final...How do you English say it...My final 'hurrah.' I'm supposed to be leaving next week."

Eliza was not terribly surprised to hear Rene was leaving. He was always talking about the wider world and his travels. But there was something about the fact that his final night as head cook at Thistlewood happened to coincide with a murder that made Eliza feel on edge—especially in light of how easy it would have been for one of the kitchen staff to have poisoned the food.

"Who's going to be head cook?" Eliza asked.

Rene shrugged. "I offered to identify a replacement—someone who would live up to my standards for your family, but your father told me to leave those issues with him. I suppose he wants to identify a successor himself."

"I heard father's been far more involved in the personnel decisions as of late. How are the new staff members working out?"

"Ah, so you know, then? I suppose it was silly of me to hide it."

"You should know that Thistlewood never keeps its secrets from me, Rene." Eliza said, though, in truth, she hadn't the slightest clue what Rene was talking about. But, if there was something hidden, she wanted to know, especially if it could shed any light on the backdrop to Lord Darlington's murder, and she knew Rene was far more likely to let something slip if he thought that she knew everything already.

Rene let out a deep sigh, one that carried with it a great deal of stress and anxiety—two things Rene usually avoided at all costs. Eliza wasn't sure what was going on, but she was certain it was nothing good.

"The new staff have been abysmal," he said with resignation. "I have no idea why we got rid of the previous staff if we were going to just replace them with this incompetent lot!"

"Does father know how bad things are? Perhaps he would—"

"—Mademoiselle, I pleaded with your father to keep my sous chef on, but he simply would not listen. He reduced my entire kitchen staff from seven cooks to just me and two young chaps from Winchester brought in to offer assistance."

"But surely you must have had a full complement of staff in the kitchen last night?"

"But of course!" Rene groaned. "But they were only temporary, I'm afraid. And the pressure of doing everything on my own was simply too much. With no adequate assistance in the kitchen, I could not be expected to keep our standards up, which is why I offered my

81

resignation. Your father asked me to stay on for the Darlington dinner. It was clearly important to him, and he agreed to take on some temporary staff to assist, so I agreed, but it has not been easy, Mademoiselle. It has not been easy at all."

"About these new staff, Rene," Eliza said, moving closer as she spoke and lowering her voice. "Can you vouch for them? Do you think they're trustworthy?"

Rene shrugged again. "I couldn't even tell you most of their names, let alone what sort of character they have. Why? You don't think they had something to do with Darlington's death, do you?"

"Wouldn't you rather it was someone you didn't know than someone you did?"

Rene thought on this for a moment.

"Well, I never saw anything untoward last night, but we were so busy, it is possible, I suppose. What does the new Inspector think? Surely, he doesn't think it was my food that did it!"

Eliza furrowed her brow. 'I've yet to meet him. I hope he's not as dour as Salisbury.'

"Or as eager as his sidekick, Phillips," Rene said. "He nearly ate all the cake by himself last night, and he's been hovering around the kitchen today looking for more scraps. I am not a food dispenser!"

Eliza laughed.

"Did any of the staff seem strange to you last night?"

Rene shook his head no, but Eliza knew him too well. She could always tell when he wasn't being straight with her.

"What is it, Rene? And don't bother lying to me. We both know I'll find out."

"You never were one to let anyone of the hook, were you Mademoiselle?" Rene said with a laugh.

"There is a maid—Molly," he continued. "She was...how you say? Out of sorts? But I'm certain it had nothing to do with the murder."

"What makes you think that? Do you know something?"

"That is Molly's business, and I'm not sure I should break her confidence even to you, Mademoiselle Eliza."

"Because she's pregnant?" Eliza said, taking the chance that the girl he was referring to was the same girl that she had encountered, first in her room and then out in the darkness of the estate, hiding in the bushes talking to someone.

Rene raised an eyebrow, a flicker of discomfort in his eyes. "It seems you were right, Mademoiselle. Thistlewood does keep no secrets from you. Yes, Molly is, how do you say? With child? Yes. But she is a good person. I am certain she had nothing to do with the murder."

"And you know Molly well?" Eliza asked. She knew Rene was confident, but Eliza couldn't help but think that there might be something here. Something that would get her to the truth of what happened to Lord Darlington.

"She has only been with us for a short time, but her father was a cook. Even though she was hired as a maid, she visits the kitchen often, and we've bonded. We've even shared some old stories and recipes. It is why she felt she could confide in me about her predicament."

"And the father? Who is he?"

"I do not know, and I do not wish to know. I do not wish to be burdened with his identity."

"Burdened?"

"Why, of course. If it is the…caliber of individual I suspect, then I would be moved to protect Molly and, in doing so, threaten not only my reputation but perhaps my ability to work in England again."

"I see," Eliza said, looking at Rene with curiosity. "Help a gal out, would you dear? What do you mean by 'caliber'?"

"I am afraid I have said too much. Forgive me. These are merely suspicions, and I do not wish to be the source of idle gossip."

"Oh, come on, Rene. Idle gossip can be fun if you give it a try."

Rene let out a loud laugh, shaking his head at Eliza head with a smile. "Ah, Mademoiselle, I have missed you—"

Before Rene could utter another word, Lady Montagu appeared in the doorway. Eliza was reasonably sure that it was the first time her mother had even so much as set foot in a kitchen, and both she and Rene were stunned into silence.

"Well don't just stand there with your mouth hanging open like a fish, dear," Lady Montagu said. "Obviously, if I've deigned to come all the way down here, the situation is quite urgent. Come along."

She turned to leave, but Eliza did not move. She was too busy trying to process what was happening.

"Is something wrong?" she asked.

"Inspector Abernathy wishes to speak to you at once," her mother said, as she began marching out of the kitchen—so confident Eliza would be following her that she did not even turn around to check. "We mustn't keep him waiting."

Eliza rarely agreed with her mother, but in this instance, she knew that she was right. Before she left, though, she had one more thing she needed to do.

She crossed over to Rene and gave him a big hug.

"Best of luck, Old Chap," she said.

"And to you, Mademoiselle."

Eliza began walking, but Rene's voice stopped her.

"Just remember. Your family is not the only one with staff, my dear. It never pays to look through too narrow a lens."

The moment he said it, Eliza knew that he was right. The Darlingtons had brought a slew of servants with them as well, and any one of them could have been the killer. She needed to speak with them immediately, but she knew she had to meet with the Inspector first—and she had to get this meeting right. She already had one law enforcement officer who suspected her of murder. If Inspector Abernathy thought that she was guilty too, Eliza could very well wind up being arrested for the death of Lord Darlington. And if she was, life as she knew it would officially be over.

CHAPTER SIXTEEN

Inspector Abernathy had been set up in Eliza's least favorite room in the house—a study she often referred to as the "ghost study." It had been designed by a man named Thomas, and as a child, Eliza believed it was haunted by his ghost and avoided it at all costs. Even now, the thought of entering the room made her shudder, and not just because she knew the Inspector was waiting for her on the other side.

Hell's bells, Eliza, pull yourself together, she thought, as she shook off her dread, straightened her dress, and raised her fist to knock on the thick oak door.

Before she could even begin knocking, a muffled voice came from inside. "Don't stand there all day on my account," it said. "Please, come in."

There was something about that voice. Something familiar. But she couldn't quite put her finger on it.

Eliza did as she was told and opened the door. The old oak creaked as it slowly swung open, and Eliza was struck, once again, by just how unpleasant this room was. It bore no resemblance to the warm, cozy affair that was her father's main study on the other side of the house. Empty bookcases lined the walls, and there was no fireplace here. Thomas had apparently insisted on that. He believed heat made a person comfortable, and comfort, he said, was why the British Empire would eventually fall. Deep down, Eliza thought there was wisdom to that, though, right now, she would have given anything for the comfort of a roaring fire and the smell of old, leather books. Anything to make the moment feel less cold and overwhelming.

"Inspector Abernathy, a pleasure to meet you," Eliza said as she closed the door behind her.

She tried to get a good look at the Inspector, but the tall, narrow window behind Abernathy backlit him in such a way that he seemed perpetually bathed in shadow. Eliza squinted slightly in hopes of bringing him into focus as she stepped forward and held out her hand.

"I'm Eliza Montagu, Lord Montagu's eldest daughter. I wish I were welcoming you to Thistlewood House under better auspices."

"Not chasing any trains today, I hope?" Inspector Abernathy said, his voice smooth yet commanding as he walked out from behind the desk and smiled as he took Eliza's hand.

At first, Eliza was flummoxed by this. It was one of those moments where the brain hides important information from you. A familiar face. A past event. But she did not have to search her memory for long to find the answer.

"You're the good chap who caught me running for the train at Kings Cross!" Eliza exclaimed as an enormous sense of relief fluttered over her. It was as though she had a connection to him, albeit a brief one, and that was enough to break the ice.

"Yes, indeed. Fascinating that our paths should cross again so quickly."

Abernathy was as handsome as he was courteous. His blond hair was no longer slicked back in a casual style. It was put into a more refined side shed, no doubt to invoke a feeling of professionalism, but his white shirt was rolled up at the sleeves, and his black suit jacket hung over the shoulders of the chair behind the desk. His tie was slightly askew.

Eliza recognized something in the look of the man immediately. He was someone who was trying desperately to fit into the expectations of Society but doing so reluctantly.

Just like me, Eliza thought.

"Please, would you have a seat?" Abernathy asked, pointing to a seat in front of the table.

"Scottish?" Eliza asked.

"It's a fair cop," Abernathy said with a smile as he sat back down in front of the window.

"We used to holiday in the Highlands. Where are you from?" Eliza asked, trying to keep the positive, cordial mood going as long as possible.

"I'm afraid I'm a Lowlands boy," Abernathy replied, as he opened up a black notepad and readied a pencil in his hand. "Glasgow to be precise."

"Oh, I've visited there as well! We went to see the shipyards, though I also slipped off early to look at Charles Rennie Mackintosh's work."

"Mackintosh, huh? So, you have an appreciation for architecture then?"

"I do—though, as much as I love his buildings, I love his watercolors more. Have you been to the Glasgow School of Art? They have a beautiful collection of his paintings on display."

"Can't say I have, Miss Montagu."

"There's no need for formalities, Inspector. You can—"

"I think, given the circumstances, it's best if we maintain a modicum of professionalism. Don't you think, Miss Montagu? After all, a man is dead."

"I'm quite aware of that, Inspector," Eliza said, her tone a bit harsher than perhaps was wise.

The Inspector had caught Eliza off guard. Abernathy was a man who could turn a warm conversation into a winter's storm in a heartbeat. Normally, Eliza was a fan of the unpredictable but not here.

"Well," Abernathy said, suddenly all charming smiles again, "Since you're here, why don't you start from the beginning."

"Of course."

Eliza knew conventional wisdom would say that compliant and demure were the right tones to strike here, but Eliza had never been one for conventional anything, and she'd be damned before she'd be demure.

"I was first conceived on a stormy November night as the owls hooted and the banshee wailed," she said with a smile.

Abernathy put down his pen and then leaned back in his chair. He stared thoughtfully at Eliza for a moment.

"You don't like authority, do you, Miss Montagu?"

"Authority is fine, darling, when it's motivated by empathy. Tell me, Inspector, are you familiar with the concept?"

"Miss Montagu, forgive me if I appear brash. It's not my intention. I am a humble working man, and I have a job to do. If you are, as you say, empathetic, surely you will assist me in making my working life not a misery?"

Eliza sighed. She found the humble working man shtick tiresome. But she also knew he was right. Her being defensive wasn't going to make this task any more enjoyable, and he had a right to want to keep a professional approach in such a dire situation.

"I apologize, Inspector. Please, ask your questions."

Abernathy sat forward and began to look over some notes. It quickly became clear to Eliza that it was the statement she had given to Salisbury.

"Salisbury doesn't like you, does he?"

"I gathered that from the way he wanted to lock up anyone here who isn't working class."

"He's a jagged fellow, Salisbury. You shouldn't take that personally. And he does have a right to suspect you. Take your statement, for example. Why did Lord Darlington wave for you to follow him out of the marquee shortly before he died?"

Eliza was unnerved. She thought back to the marquee, and he was right. Lord Darlington had beckoned her just as he was leaving so that they could have some time in private: But how would he know that?

Her heart started racing. Ollie. She had tried to use Lord Darlington's clear signal for her to go off with him to make him jealous. He must have told the Inspector.

Eliza felt foolish. She should have mentioned Lord Darlington's request when she met with Salisbury. Now it looked like a serious omission—the type someone would make if they were trying to cover up their guilt.

"That's right," Eliza finally said, doing her best to seem surprised. "Now that I think of it, he did beckon me to follow him. But I did not. I'm certain everyone in the marquee will vouch for that."

"Yes, of course..." Abernathy said, pausing for what seemed to Eliza an eternity before continuing, "And I suppose that was the last contact you had with him? A final wave goodbye from across the room?"

"Absolutely."

The moment the word came out of her mouth, Eliza knew that it wasn't true. There was one other point of contact. She hadn't intended to lie—it just hadn't immediately come to mind, probably due to the stress of the situation and the fact that the last point of contact wasn't a conversation. She knew she needed to correct herself, and she opened her mouth to do just that, but the Inspector didn't let her get that far. He had obviously been ready for her denial, stalking it like a tiger waiting to strike.

"That's funny," he said. "Because one of the servants, a boy named Frank, said he passed a note to you directly from Lord Darlington. As it happens, he isn't very good at being discreet, this Frank. He's actually very good at reading notes not written for his eyes and then telling the authorities all about them."

In her mind's eye, Eliza could see the words of that note, staring up at her from her open hand:

Eliza, meet me in your room away from prying eyes and ears. There is something I need to tell you.

"Our dear little Frank can't remember the exact words, but he was certain Darlington was asking to see you privately so he could tell you something important."

The room fell silent. A light breeze taunted the window behind Abernathy with portions of dust and gravel from outside. The pitter-patter sounded to Eliza like fingers trying to make their way into the room. Fingers that were not benevolent, which seemed fitting, given the circumstances.

"Miss Montagu," Abernathy said, searching her face with his deep blue eyes. "A man had something important to tell you, he wanted to see you in private, and now he is dead. It appears to me that you have some explaining to do, do you not?"

"I know how it looks, Inspector, but I assure you, I have no idea what he was going to tell me. All I know is that he was interested in me romantically, and he wanted to prove that he wasn't as stuck up as he had appeared at dinner."

"It's convenient that you don't know what he was going to say in private, Miss Montagu."

"Perhaps. But it is also the truth."

Abernathy stared at her for a moment before standing up and pointing to the door.

"We can continue this conversation later, Miss Montagu. I am, if nothing else, sporting. Perhaps by then you will have come up with a more believable story than 'I don't know what he was going to say.'"

"Don't you want the rest of my statement?"

"It may be unorthodox, Miss Montagu, but I believe a murder is like a jigsaw puzzle. It must be put together carefully and with thought. Furiously trying to find the right pieces only impedes the solving of the puzzle. One piece at a time, and the truth will out."

Eliza left the room feeling like a fuse had been lit. Abernathy was tenacious, and he would want to know the truth behind Darlington's note. Without that truth, it was easy to see how the Inspector could suspect Eliza of murder. The possibility that she killed Lord Darlington to silence him from spreading some unpalatable truth was an obvious trail for him to follow.

But Eliza had her own trail to follow. One that was currently taking her directly to Lord Darlington's servants—and, hopefully, Lord Darlington's killer.

CHAPTER SEVENTEEN

Abernathy had flustered Eliza. He was both charming and accusatory, which Eliza found to be a potent mix. He had the potential to be either savior or devil, and she hoped beyond hope that he was the former.

At least he is fair, Eliza thought as she walked the hallways of the ground floor. *Unlike that Salisbury fellow.*

As Eliza walked down to the first floor, she took stock of what she knew so far. This was something she had done since she was a child. A problem would be seen in her mind as a painting, a great work of art that was impeded by an inherent flaw. She had seen paintings like that before at exhibitions in London. She had even painted a few mistakes in her time.

Those paintings were a strange thing to Eliza. You could immediately feel that something was "off" about them, but it was only through careful analysis that you could determine what that problem was. It could be a shadow in the wrong place, a color that was a little too saturated, or even an object or part of a person that was ever so slightly out of proportion.

When Eliza was training herself as a painter, she would stare at a work with an inherent flaw for hours. She would observe it carefully, and then, she would close her eyes and envision the painting, making note of every slight subtlety and detail. Then, she would pull it apart in her mind and look for the flaw. Piece by piece, the painting would reveal its layers and complexities until, finally, Eliza would discover the culprit—the mistake that ruined the work of art.

As she went in search of Darlington's servants, Eliza was doing just that, though this time, what she was dissecting was a different sort of image—one of a man dead on her bedroom floor, surrounded in her mind by the possible killers. So far, Barnsley's image was the sharpest, him standing there with a sneer. But coming into focus were the servants. They too had the opportunity, and, if his behavior at dinner the previous evening was any indication, they likely also had plenty of motive.

Let's see what his own servants thought of him, Eliza thought as she reached the Admiral's Hallway.

The Admiral's Hallway was a special place in Thistlewood House. It was the place Lord Montagu always housed his guests. Other than the master bedroom, the rooms situated in the Admiral's Hallway were the best in the house.

The hallway itself was named after Admiral Kent, a navy Admiral who had owned Thistlewood House in the seventeenth century. Before taking over Thistlewood House, he spent time as a pirate hunter in the New World colonies, a detail that had utterly enthralled Eliza as a child.

Eliza walked past the most luxurious rooms, their large, pristinely polished oak doors closed to the world, and continued on towards the servant's section. As was the way, the servant chambers for esteemed guests were situated on another hallway that turned right at the end of the corridor. This corridor had no name. The servants were not given the privilege of it.

Not only were these rooms anonymous, but they were also small and cramped, as though fitted in as an afterthought. Eliza had always been frustrated by the stark difference in opulence between the rooms in the Admiral's Hallway and the servant chambers. She was a firm believer that simply having a title did not entitle one to better treatment, and she wished her house did not so obviously suggest otherwise.

Eliza padded softly down the carpeted hall as she searched for a clue. Thankfully, it presented itself swiftly in the sound of a thump from behind the fourth door down the hall. Eliza approached it, readied herself, and knocked.

The woman who answered the door cut a graven image. She was in her forties, so youth had not completely left her, but any spark certainly had. Her eyes were dull with dark patches beneath them, making it clear to Eliza that the woman had hardly slept. And who could blame her after the night they'd had?

"Yes?"

"I'm sorry to trouble you," Eliza began. "I'm—"

"We know who you are," the woman interrupted.

A young man, no more than twenty years of age, pulled the door open further. He was standing over the woman, his face twisted into an expression of deep distrust.

"Is this her, then?" he asked.

"It is indeed," the woman replied.

"Well, ma'am, we don't need you comin' around here giving us no comis…comis…commiserations.'"

"'Condolences, son,'" the woman interrupted. "You be a good boy and keep packing. I'll deal with this."

Eliza felt awful. The servants had already been through a great deal in the last twenty-four hours, and she could tell her presence was making things worse.

"I really mean no intrusion," she said, hoping to put their mind at ease. "I was just hoping to talk with some of Lord Darlington's servants for a moment."

"We ain't his servants no more, are we!?" the man said loudly from inside the room, pulling around a large, brown luggage trunk.

"Quiet!" the woman snapped with a seething whisper. She then beckoned Eliza into her room, shutting the door behind her.

Eliza looked around and saw that the tiny room was being used to store clothes and other items. Most of these, the man was trying to force into the trunk.

"I don't want to disturb you, ma'am," Eliza assured her. "It will only take a minute."

The woman gave Eliza a stare that made her blood run cold. Even at the suffragette marches, she'd never had anyone stare at her with that level of hatred.

"The only reason I've brought you in here, Miss Montagu, is out of courtesy for our Lady Darlington, so as we don't disturb her. We know well and good what you did to Lord Darlington."

"Watch her, Mum," the man said as he folded a white nightshirt and placed it into the overflowing trunk. "She already k…k…killed the Lord. Who knows what she's goin' to do now?"

The only thing that travelled faster than gossip was suspicion, and clearly, the suspicion surrounding Eliza was moving at an accelerated pace. Usually, she would have risen up to any accusation, but here that would have only gotten in the way. It was hard, but solving this murder was far more important than defending her name, so she took a diplomatic tone instead.

"I didn't kill anyone," she said softly. "But I do wish to find out who did. For all our sakes."

"K…Killers always say 'at!" the man said, folding his arms and waiting for a response.

"Someone poisoned Lord Darlington, and I want to find out who," Eliza continued calmly. "Whether you like it or not, the servants, both those we employ and those employed by the Darlingtons, will be likely suspects."

"What've we ever done!" the man shrieked.

"We're servants. Access to the Lord's cup and plate. We could have done it any time," the woman answered.

"I can see you are an intelligent woman," Eliza said, "so I suspect you know I'm right. And the fastest way to ensure you don't get accidentally caught up in a murder investigation is to help me find the person who did this. Please, if you saw anything suspicious that night—anything out of the ordinary before Lord Darlington's murder—"

"We didn't see nothin' suspicious," the man insisted. But the mother—she looked pensive. Eliza could tell there was something on her mind, and she was desperate to draw it out of her. Whatever it was could be the key to clearing her name and keeping her family out of Abernathy's crosshairs.

"I suspect your mother here can speak for herself," Eliza said, hoping that employing a bit of feminism might be enough to get the woman to open up.

Luckily for Eliza, her instincts were correct.

"I didn't see nothin' out of the ordinary before, but after…"

"After what?" Eliza asked, trying to contain her excitement. "What did you see after?"

"It's more what I didn't see. Or, more precisely who I didn't see."

"Mother—" the son said, clearly concerned that she was about to give away something important—a cue that caused Eliza's heart to fill with hope.

"Hush, boy," she said harshly. "Don't you have packing to do?"

A slight flush rose into the son's cheeks, and he looked away, embarrassed. He quickly embarked on a futile quest to punch a pair of trousers into the full-to-bursting trunk as the mother turned her attention to Eliza.

"Lord Darlington's head valet went missing just after the murder, ma'am. No one has seen him since."

At first blush, this seemed like wonderful news to Eliza. At last, she had a promising suspect. Things were starting to look up! But then, she was struck by a terrible thought. What if the valet hadn't gone missing because he was trying to hide from the police? What if he was missing because he, too, had been murdered?

And if the killer had already claimed two victims, what were the chances someone Eliza loved would be next?

CHAPTER EIGHTEEN

Eliza wasn't sure where to begin her search for the valet, but she was sure where she wanted to go next. The kitchen. She always thought more clearly when she wasn't hungry, and there was something about being around Rene when he was cooking that she always found soothing. And, truth be told, right now she could use something soothing. Something delicious wouldn't hurt either.

So, she grabbed Scout and followed the smell of warm cinnamon to the kitchen, where she stood beside Rene as he made a stunning Tarte Tatin. She watched hungrily as he added the perfectly quartered apples to the rich, bubbling caramel on the stove. She had always loved Rene's Tarte Tatin, so much so that she had even asked him to teach her to make it once. It was an unusual sight—the daughter of a Lord galivanting around in the kitchen—but Eliza had always been an unusual girl.

"You could help if you'd like," Rene said. He was usually very protective of his bakes, but he had a soft spot for Eliza. Plus, the fact that Tarte Tatins were supposed to be rustic meant it would be impossible for her to muck up his presentation.

"Eliza?" Rene said when he did not get a response. "Eliza!"

"I'm so sorry. I was…distracted."

"By the Tarte or something else?"

"Both," Eliza replied.

"Very well. I made some scones for tea. Would you like me to get you one? You could eat it while you tell me all about whatever it is that has you so distracted."

"I can get them. You had best not take your eyes of that caramel. A wise man once taught me that," Eliza said with a wink as she crossed over to the larder.

She grabbed a scone, a small container of clotted cream, and some fresh blueberry jam and carried them over to the counter beside Rene. She slathered the scone liberally with both cream and jam and took a bite.

"I take it the scone is to your liking, m'lady?"

"It is the bee's knees, Rene," Eliza replied.

And it was. The scone had just the right texture—crumbly and soft but not too dry—and the richness of the clotted cream combined with the tartness of the blueberries came together to form the perfect bite.

"Good. Now, tell me, what is it that's got you so distracted?"

"Lord Darlington's valet. One of the servants told me he hasn't been seen since the murder was discovered. That's suspicious, don't you think?"

"Perhaps," Rene said. "Though I would hope you would have substantially more evidence than that before making any sort of accusation."

"Of course. That's why I want to find him. Assuming he can be found, of course. Assuming he's not…"

"Dead? Really, Eliza. I expect this sort of catastrophizing from Lady Montagu, but you? You've always been the one to keep your wits about you."

Rene was right, of course. It was far more likely that the servant had disappeared because he was involved somehow. Plus, they'd already had one murder on the property. What were the odds that they would have a second one in less than twenty-four hours?

Eliza watched as Rene draped the buttery pastry gently over the top of the apples. She was always so awed by his skills. Hers never laid perfectly the way that his did. He was a true artist in the kitchen, and there was something about watching his gentle precision that felt almost meditative to Eliza.

Eliza took a moment to relish being right. The kitchen was absolutely the correct place for her to go. She felt calmer already.

"I just wish I knew how to find him—" Eliza began, but before she could finish her sentence, she was interrupted by Scout, who whined softly at her feet.

"I just wish you had not found it appropriate to bring that thing into my kitchen."

"Oh, Rene, don't be such a curmudgeon! Just look at his face! Besides, you cannot fault him for wanting some of your delicious scones."

With that, Eliza broke off a small piece of the scone and slipped it to Scout, who devoured it eagerly.

"If only I could speak with him…" she said, as she watched Scout sniff the floor for any residual crumbs.

"The valet?"

"Yes. If I could just speak with him, I suspect I could, at the very least, uncover something that will help us get to the truth of the matter.

But that will only prove possible if I can locate him, and I am not sure how I am to do that if no one knows where he is."

Scout once again whined at Eliza's feet.

"That's quite enough," she said gently. "I understand you liked the scone, but there is no need to get greedy about it."

"That's the problem with these old houses," Eliza continued, returning her attention to Rene and jumping back to the topic at hand. "They are so large that one could hide in them for months without ever being seen by another person. If the valet is determined to stay hidden here, I am not sure there is a person alive who could find him."

Scout whined again, more insistently this time.

"Perhaps not a person…" Rene began.

"But perhaps someone else could!" Eliza grinned as she leaned down and scratched Scout between his ears before picking up his leash.

"Come along, Scout. I have a mission for you."

***

Even though Eliza knew that no one was there, she still found herself knocking on the door when she arrived at the servant's quarters where Lord Darlington's valet had been staying. To do any differently felt impolite and disrespectful, and neither of those were adjectives Eliza wanted the servants to associate with her.

When the third knock went unanswered, she slipped the key—given to her by Parkins under protest—into the lock and gently eased open the door. The room it revealed was small and housed only a single bed in a stark, black bedframe; a wooden dresser; and a chipped pitcher of water. Her mother would never, ever have allowed something like that to be placed in a Lord or Lady's room. The mere suggestion of chipped porcelain being allowed in one of their guest's quarters would have been sufficient to justify their firing. However, in the servants' rooms, apparently, her mother did not care if the pitchers were worse for wear.

The advantage of the room being so small was that Eliza could investigate it quickly. It took no time at all for her to identify the valet's suitcase—a small, black box stashed under the bed—and pull it out. Thankfully, there was no lock, so Eliza had no trouble whatsoever getting it open.

She felt a bit guilty going through the man's things like this, but she reminded herself that it was for the greater good. There was a murderer on the loose, and the Constable was looking in all the wrong places. If she discontinued her investigation just because things made her uncomfortable, it was likely that no one would ever get to the truth, and that was something Eliza simply could not abide.

Gingerly, she lifted a sock from the man's suitcase and held it down to Scout, who somehow seemed to understand exactly what Eliza wanted and began sniffing it immediately.

"Now, I know you're too small to make a proper hunting dog, but that does not mean you don't have proper hunting instincts," Eliza began. She had planned to say more, but before she could utter another word, Scout had taken off, nose pressed firmly to the ground. She had to race to grab the end of his leash before he disappeared.

Scout dragged Eliza through the labyrinth of hallways and out into the garden, where he nearly ran Eliza straight into her mother.

"Good heavens, Eliza," she said, thoroughly startled. "You must control your creature!"

Eliza was still considering the appropriate response when Scout pulled the leash harder, dragging her away from the rose bushes her mother was carefully tending and into the perfectly manicured hedge maze.

"No end to your usefulness, I see," Eliza said with a laugh as Scout guided her through the maze and out into the topiary garden.

Eliza struggled to keep up as Scout, suddenly all business, led her past the stunning fountain that was the centerpiece of that section of the garden before leading her by a majestic weeping willow alongside a small stream.

Awfully strange for him to have come all the way out here, Eliza thought, as she followed Scout into a forest near the edge of the property. *I cannot fathom any official business that would necessitate it.*

"Are you sure, Scout?" Eliza asked.

Though he did not audibly reply, the fact that he pressed his nose even closer to the ground and further picked up the pace seemed to Eliza like a pretty clear answer.

It wasn't until they were at least a kilometer into the forest that it occurred to Eliza just how dangerous what she was doing could turn out to be. After all, she had come out into the woods, alone and unarmed, in search of a murder suspect. What was she going to do if she found him?

Before Eliza could even begin to think that thought all the way through, she heard the unmistakable sound of rustling leaves beside her. Something was nearby, and judging from the sound of it, whatever it was was big.

Eliza's heart caught in her throat.

I should have brought one of father's hunting rifles, she thought. She would never have used it, of course. Eliza was an excellent shot, but ever since she was a little girl, she had refused to aim at anything other than clay pigeons. Still, the valet didn't have to know that, and she suspected the mere sight of the rifle would have been enough to keep him from any funny business. Not that it mattered now, as she didn't have it with her regardless.

Eliza held her breath as a figure emerged from the bushes, and she laughed out loud when she realized that the thing she'd been so frightened of was not a man but rather, a peacock.

"You gave me quite a scare!" she said as the peacock wandered slowly past her, its stunning feathers fanned out to fully display its magnificent design.

Unfazed, the peacock simply let out a squawk before continuing on.

Eliza laughed again.

"Crickey, Scout! I can't believe I got myself all in a tizzy about something as silly as a peacock."

Just then, Eliza turned the corner, and suddenly found herself face-to-face with something much less silly than a peacock. Something that looked an awful lot like very real danger.

There, less than ten feet in front of her, was a man, presumably Lord Darlington's valet, holding a shovel and staring right at her.

CHAPTER NINETEEN

"Hello?" the valet said, surprised.

"Hello, there," Eliza replied. "I'm sorry to interrupt."

"That's quite alright."

It was clear that he was baffled by her presence, but his training made him too polite to question her directly. At least, not without making some small talk first.

Eliza wasn't sure what to do. She'd given a great deal of thought to finding the valet but very little thought to what she would do if she did, and she realized in this moment what a mistake that was. After all, she could not simply come out and ask him if he was the murderer. She needed a plan, and she absolutely did not have one.

"You're Lady Eliza, yes? Lord Montagu's daughter?"

Eliza nodded.

"Liam O'Conner," he said with a stiff, little bow. "I'm Lord Darlington's man."

"Pleased to meet you," Eliza replied. She couldn't help but notice his use of present tense there, and she wondered if that linguistic slip was indicative of anything—if there was something she could glean from the fact that, even after his death, he still viewed himself as Lord Darlington's man.

"What are you doing out here?" he asked before Eliza could finish considering his word choice.

Eliza froze for a moment. Apparently, a good cover story was yet another thing she had forgotten to come up with before she followed Scout out here.

"I could ask you the same thing," she said in an effort to buy time.

"Yes, but I asked you first."

"Yes," she said, cocking her head slightly to the right and infusing her voice and demeanor with the same sense of confidence she used with the men at the suffragette marches. "But you're the one with the shovel."

"Fair," Liam said, laughing.

The laugh should have been comforting, but Eliza couldn't help but notice that the smile that accompanied it never quite reached his eyes.

More importantly, the shovel never left his hand. She was starting to think that she might really be in trouble. But she wasn't about to let that stop her.

Eliza waited, expecting him to offer an explanation any moment, but that moment never came. If she was going to get anywhere, clearly, she was going to have to change tact.

"I'm terribly sorry about Lord Darlington's passing. Had you known him long?"

"Yes. I started working for the family as soon as I was of age and worked my way up to head valet. I've been with him almost ten years now."

"His death must have come as quite a shock."

"Indeed."

Eliza studied his face. He looked tired—the sort of tired you feel in both your body and your soul. But whether he was tired because he was grieving or tired because he was carrying the weight of a murder on his conscience, that she couldn't say for sure. At least, not yet.

Clearly, getting to the bottom of this was going to require her to push a little harder.

"But perhaps also a relief," she said, tentatively testing the waters. "After all, I saw how he treated the servants. He had some very old-fashioned views. Views which, I assure you, I do not share."

Liam laughed at that, too, which Eliza found thoroughly confusing.

"I'm sorry, m'lady," he said, his eyes fixed on the base of his shovel so as to avoid her gaze. "It's just—well, we all heard that. You and your little outburst were the talk of the servant's quarters last night. At least, until…"

"…Until the murder."

"Yes."

Again, there was silence between them. Liam leaned against a nearby tree, and Eliza wondered how long he'd been out here digging in the heat. She had to imagine he was thirsty, and she wished she'd had the foresight to think about bringing water with her. That way, she could have offered him some.

Mother's training runs deep, she thought with an internal chuckle. *Even when staring down a potential murderer, I am nothing if not a gracious hostess.*

Scout growled quietly beside her.

Back to the matter at hand, Eliza, she reminded herself.

"With the way he treated you, I wouldn't blame you at all if you wanted him dead," she said, deciding to just jump in and see what sort of reaction she could provoke.

And provoke a reaction she did. Suddenly, Liam's entire demeanor changed. His eyes flashed with fury, and Eliza's heart quickened as she noticed the way his knuckles went white as he gripped the shovel tighter.

"Wait a minute!" he cried, outraged and indignant. "You think I did this, don't you? That's why you've come out here! So you can see if I'm some sort of murderer!"

In truth, that was exactly why she'd done it, but she wasn't about to tell him that. Not with the way he was holding that shovel.

"Don't be absurd. I was simply taking the dog out for a stroll, and he led me here. It gets awfully stuffy in the house this time of year, and—"

"Forgive me, m'lady, but while I may not be rich, I am also not stupid."

Eliza was as taken aback by his bluntness as by the accusation.

"I'm sorry," she said. And she meant it. Killer or not, she never wanted anyone to think that she was judging their intelligence based on their social class, and she was horrified by the thought that she had done so here.

"Lord Darlington was not the man you thought he was, Lady. And even if he was, I would never have killed him! What motive would I have? With him gone, the family has no reason to keep me on. I'll lose my job and have no choice but to go work for another family—one where I'm likely to be treated far worse. And that's assuming I can even find another job. People are unlikely to be quick to hire a head valet whose Lord was murdered on their watch. The suspicion alone…"

"I really am sorry. Truly. I hadn't thought about it like that," Eliza said.

She was ashamed by just how true that statement was. As much as she had tried to carve her own path and move away from the social conventions of her childhood, the truth was that sometimes she was still blinded by it. That was why she had failed to consider the impact Lord Darlington's murder would have on Liam's job security and how that would function as a mitigating factor. She couldn't help but wonder what other important things her privileged upbringing had prevented her from considering.

"Lord Darlington was a good man," Liam said. "Much of what he said was just bluster. He was keeping up appearances."

Liam sat down on a nearby stump. It was clear that this exchange had exhausted him, but he felt compelled to continue—to defend Lord Darlington. Eliza had never felt so guilty.

"The truth is, Lord Darlington was in love with a servant girl."

Eliza stared at him, stunned by this revelation. Liam was right. She had most definitely misjudged Lord Darlington.

But this also meant Lord Darlington was carrying a very big secret. And where one secret was, others often followed. And any one of those secrets could have been enough to get him killed.

"He wanted to be with her," Liam continued, "but his family would never allow it. There was too much resting on his shoulders. The business. Their legacy. Foolish as it was, he thought if he could make a change—something big and substantial enough that the family would never again have to worry about money or status—maybe then he would have enough cover to be with the woman he loved. So, he took a risk with the family's business. A big one."

"And?" Eliza asked, desperate for Liam to finish the story. There was a clue here, something that would help her figure out what happened to Lord Darlington. She could feel it. She just needed him to hurry up and share it.

"It failed. Quite spectacularly, actually. It would take a miracle to save it at this point, which is why Lord Darlington agreed to dinner with you. He was hoping you might be his miracle. He had hoped that a merger between your two families would be enough to salvage the business. More than that, he was hoping that, based on how progressive you are, you might be open to a—"

He paused for a moment, and Eliza could tell he was trying to figure out how to phrase something delicately. She also knew he would not be putting this level of thought into his word choice if she were a man, which was something she'd always resented. She wasn't some sort of delicate flower in need of protection, especially from something as innocuous as words.

"Spit it out, O'Conner," she said. "I assure you, there will be nothing you say here that I haven't heard before—and likely even said myself at some stage."

"Of course. Forgive me," Liam said before clearing his throat and continuing on.

"He was hoping you might be open to an...alternate arrangement. One wherein you two would marry to keep up appearances, but you could maintain your life in London, and he could maintain...well...her."

Eliza couldn't help but laugh at that. He certainly wasn't mincing words now.

"I take it that's why he wanted me to meet him privately? So he could explain things?"

"Yes. So, you see, Lady Eliza, I had no reason to kill him. Not only was he my employer, but he was also my friend."

"I see. I am terribly sorry for your loss. And I promise, I will do everything I can to help find the person who killed him and ensure they are brought to justice."

"Thank you."

"This issue with the business—that could be motive. Who all was aware of his struggles?"

"No one. Just me, and I came out here today to ensure it stayed that way."

With that, Liam produced a notebook from his bag.

"Is that a ledger?" Eliza asked, squinting at it slightly.

"Yes. It is the only proof of Lord Darlington's misstep with the business. I wanted to make sure his secrets died with him."

"You're a good man, O'Conner."

"Thank you, m'lady."

"But I can't let you do that. That ledger is essential for the running of the family's business. If you truly want to honor his legacy, you won't destroy the only thing they could use to save it."

Liam stared at her for a moment, and Eliza could tell he was wrestling with this perspective. What she'd said was obviously true, but it was also completely at odds with his protective instincts.

"You're right m'lady," he said finally. "Thank you."

"Promise me you'll take that directly to Jacob Darlington."

"I will, m'lady. I promise."

"Excellent. No need to hang around here then. Why don't you accompany me back?"

"I would be honored, m'lady."

Eliza's head was spinning as she, Scout, and Liam walked back to the estate. She had learned so much during her conversation with Liam, and yet, somehow, she was no closer to solving Darlington's murder now than she was when she'd started out here. In fact, if anything, she was further away.

She had to find a new clue and fast. Otherwise, she was beginning to think she might spend the rest of her life in jail for a murder she did not commit.

CHAPTER TWENTY

Eliza wandered through Thistlewood House wondering what to do next. She was desperate for a clue but completely at a loss for where to find one. For a moment, she thought she saw Barnsley, lurking around a corner, but when she checked the hallway she thought he'd disappeared down, there was no one there.

You're chasing ghosts, Eliza, she thought, as she headed towards the lobby and searched for a plan. She considered speaking with the servants again, but it was clear that their growing mistrust of her would make that difficult. Plus, this was not the ideal time to speak with any of them.

Though Eliza had been away from Thistlewood House for some time, it was easy to see that the old schedules remained the same. It was nearing midday and that meant the servants were on cleaning duty. Eliza's mother made sure that Parkins and the rest of the staff cleaned the most used spaces of the house between breakfast and lunch. This way, it remained presentable to anyone who might arrive in the afternoon.

For Eliza, the idea of running Thistlewood House was a boring one. She would rather explore its nooks and crannies while getting lost in its stories and history. That was where the fun was to be had, not in the administrative duties required to keep the old place from falling down. She had to admit, in that sense at least, Thistlewood was in very good hands. Her mother would make sure it was in the best of conditions, even if that meant the residents and guests were left creaking under pressure. Even on her mother's worst days, however, she had never been able to generate the level of pressure Eliza felt right now.

Eliza wandered through the main lobby and into the West side of the house. As a child, she had thought Thistlewood had a certain kind of magic, and she found herself wishing she still believed that now—that if she just looked closely enough, the house would reveal something to her. Something useful. Something that would help her change things.

Much as she wished it would, the house did not give her a clue. It did, however, provide her with an unexpected run-in with Oliver

Fairfax, who was so thoroughly distracted by his own worries that he crashed right into Eliza when rounding a corner.

"My apologies," Oliver said quickly. It was clear that he was startled. And something else too. He wore a smile upon his face, and his tweed suit was as pristine as usual, but his eyes told the real story. Eliza could tell that he was worried, and that was deeply out of character for him. She was surprised by how much it hurt her to see him look so burdened.

"Everything okay, Ollie?"

"Other than someone being murdered, you mean?"

"I know. It's surreal. I still can't believe it's happened here of all places."

"These walls have stood for hundreds of years, Liza. I'm certain this isn't the first untimely death they've witnessed, nor will it be the last."

Eliza had never seen Ollie so maudlin. She found herself overwhelmed with the desire to hug him—one she likely would have given into had they been in London. But they were not. They were in Thistlewood, and Ladies did not do such things at Thistlewood. Not even rebels like Eliza.

Ollie looked around and then stepped closer, lowering his voice. "Have you met with the Inspector, yet? I'm concerned that he may suspect you."

"I have and he does, but you needn't worry, Darling. I can handle the man." Eliza was trying to keep the mood light, but it only took one look at Ollie's face to make it clear her plan was not working.

"That's your problem, Liza," Ollie said sternly. "You always think you can handle men. He seems decent at first, but I am telling you if I ever thought the devil walked on this Earth, he would wear the Inspector's grin."

"The truth will out, Ollie. I'm sure of it. You needn't worry so much! It will give you frown lines, and we can't very well have that now, can we?"

Eliza expected Ollie to laugh at that, but he didn't. Instead, he just stared at her with affectionate, pleading eyes.

"Please, Liza," he said in a tone more serious than Eliza had ever heard from him. "Be careful. You can't always be the smartest person in the room. And I have little faith in the justice system when scandal is involved. This could turn into a witch hunt, and even the innocent could be burned at the stake."

Eliza patted Ollie on the chest with her hand. "Thank you for the concern, Ollie. But if I can handle you blowing hot and cold like the weather, I can handle the Inspector."

"I'm not so cold, am I?" Ollie said, touching Eliza's hand. There was so much warmth in the gesture, and much as she tried to stop it, Eliza's heart fluttered in response. But before she could do anything about it, they were interrupted by Cedric.

"Dear Lord!" Cedric shouted from over Ollie's shoulder. "Please be courteous with my sister, Old Bean."

Ollie stood back. The moment was gone.

"You are a master of intrusion, brother," Eliza said with a smile—though, truthfully, she could have strangled him.

"Saving you from these awful Fairfaxes," Cedric replied, giving Ollie a friendly bump with his elbow.

"It's your sister you should watch, Cedric. She's manhandling me."

Cedric pulled out his pipe and started packing it with tobacco. "Eliza wouldn't dream of such a thing," he said, his tone dripping with sarcasm.

"Cedric," Ollie asked. "Have you spoken with this Inspector Abernathy yet?"

"Only a cordial welcome when he arrived, why?"

"Ollie thinks he's the devil," Eliza joked.

"Oh dear," Cedric said as he lit his pipe. "He'll fit right in here then."

Cedric grinned before taking a deep puff of his pipe and letting the smoke curl out of his mouth, thick and sweet smelling. Eliza knew that smell well. It was the same apple cherry tobacco her father smoked.

"Have either of you seen our elusive brother? He's harder to get a hold of than God these days—keeps disappearing whenever he's needed."

Ollie and Eliza both shook their heads, and Cedric sighed wearily. "He's probably off cavorting with a lady somewhere. I think I might put a leash on him one of these days. Anyways, lovely to see you both, but I must dash," Cedric said, as he began walking towards the stairwell. But before he had even rounded the corner, Melville unexpectedly appeared.

"Speak of the devil," Ollie said.

"I thought that was Abernathy," Eliza replied with a grin.

Ollie laughed this time, though it was half-hearted and obligatory at best. Eliza had never seen him in such a state. It was deeply disconcerting.

"I'm glad you're all here," Melville said. Eliza couldn't help but note that he, too, seemed uncharacteristically serious, and she found that that made her even more anxious than Abernathy.

"I just bumped into Salisbury," Melville continued. "He and Abernathy want to see us all in the dining room at once."

"Did they discover something?" Ollie asked anxiously.

"I don't know. But there was something in his tone that..."

"That what?" Cedric asked.

"I don't know. But I think perhaps now is the time to worry."

With that, Melville turned and headed towards the parlor, with Ollie, Cedric, and Eliza in tow. As they walked, Eliza felt a chill run up her spine. She wasn't sure what Abernathy could possibly have uncovered that would have warranted summoning them all like this, but she was sure of one thing: Melville was right. Now was definitely the time to worry.

CHAPTER TWENTY ONE

The Montagus, Darlingtons, and Fairfaxes stood huddled around the enormous dining room table in the marquee under the watchful eyes of Abernathy and Salisbury. Despite the room's cavernous, open nature, somehow the whole place felt cramped—as though the walls were closing in on them.

They all stood there silently for what felt like an eternity. Eliza did her best to keep quiet, despite the fact that that was far from a natural state for her. Much as she hated the thought of being silenced, she knew Ollie was right about the need for her to be careful. Silence was bad, but prison was worse.

Eventually, though, she could bear standing there under the murderous gaze of Lady Darlington no longer, and before she could stop herself, words were spilling out of her mouth.

"So, what's all this about then?"

"I'm glad you asked, Lady Montagu," Inspector Abernathy said. "As some of you suspected, we believe Lord Darlington may have been poisoned, which makes understanding the circumstances surrounding the dinner essential to understanding the crime. In order to do that, I thought it might be helpful to have a reenactment of sorts. I know it's a bit unorthodox—"

"A bit?" Cedric whispered to Eliza, one eyebrow raised.

"—but recreating the circumstances surrounding Lord Darlington's demise may help us identify his killer. So, if you would all please take a seat at the table, being sure to arrange yourself in the same seats you sat in that evening…"

Inspector Abernathy paused, clearly expecting them to begin moving into place accordingly. It was obvious from the grumbling and snail's pace at which they moved that no one was excited about this idea, but they weren't about to say no to the Inspector.

"Well, I never," Lady Darlington said to Jacob, as he pulled her chair out for her. "A reenactment. How absurd! Once at that dinner was more than enough."

"This," Eliza said, "is one rare area on which you and I are in total agreement, Lady Darlington."

"That empty space," Inspector Abernathy said, pointing to the chair next to Eliza. "Is that where Lord Darlington sat?"

"It is," Eliza said.

"Until you killed him," Lady Darlington hissed.

"Mother! That's enough," Jacob whispered. "You can't keep making these sorts of unfounded accusations. Especially in front of law enforcement."

"I can do as I please, Jacob. I am your elder. You'd do well to remember that."

"Interesting that the deceased was seated right next to you, Lady Montagu," Salisbury said, with a grin so wide you'd think he was a cat who had just eaten a canary.

"If by interesting you mean utterly expected and sensible then yes, it is absolutely fascinating," Eliza said, thoroughly unable to keep the disdain from her voice at this point. She knew fighting with the constable was unwise, but she was endlessly tired of dealing with this man and his constant condescension and innuendo.

"What happened next?" Inspector Abernathy asked, clearly eager to keep everyone calm and on track.

"The servants brought out the starter," Cedric offered.

"Yes," Lady Darlington interjected. "Veal. A clear sign the Montagus were attempting to operate above their class. They don't even know how to prepare a proper dinner menu."

"The veal was delicious," Eliza said. "And just because it wasn't what you expected for a first course does not give you any right to go about criticizing Rene's ability to make a menu. He was one of the most renowned chefs in Paris before father brought him here, and—"

"Alright ladies," Abernathy jumped in. "Let's dispense of the culinary debate, shall we? I'm much more interested in what was said at the meal than what was served."

"That was also far below the quality one would expect from a family in this station," Lady Darlington replied. "Eliza—"

"—Please, Lady Darlington. My friends call me Eliza. I think it would best if you stuck with Lady Montagu."

"Eliza!" Great Aunt Martha chided.

"I heard there was some sort of outburst," Inspector Abernathy said.

"I would hardly call it an outburst," Eliza replied. She hated the use of words like "outburst." It played into this narrative of the "hysterical woman," and Eliza was anything but that.

"Lady Montagu and Lord Darlington had a mild tête-à-tête over his treatment of the servants, but it hardly constitutes a motive for murder," Ollie said, eager to come to Eliza's rescue.

"We'll be the judge of that," Salisbury countered.

"Well, then you should be suspicious of me as well," Ollie said. "I agreed with Eliza's views on Darlington's attitude towards the help. I found them repugnant. And the servants—certainly no one had more cause for anger than they did. Have you spoken with them like this?"

"The servants are not our concern right now," Salisbury replied.

"Well, perhaps they should be," Ollie said. The men stared at each other fiercely for a moment.

Eliza found herself surprised. This, too, was completely out of character for Ollie. Between this, his unexpected anxiety, and his genuineness with her in the corridor, Eliza was beginning to feel as though she hardly knew who he was anymore.

"So, after the 'tête-à-tête' as you call it," Abernathy said, once more trying to get the conversation back on track, "What happened next?"

"Oliver suggested we take a walk," Eliza replied.

"And then what?"

"And then we took a walk," Eliza said flatly.

Abernathy rolled his eyes.

"What happened at the dinner?"

"We ate," Great Aunt Martha said curtly. It was clear she, too, was growing tired of this exercise.

"Did anyone else leave?"

"Great Aunt Martha came to get Oliver and I once my absence had been deemed more unbecoming than my presence," Eliza said. "And though he was never at the party, Barnsley was wandering about during the dinner, which certainly seems worth noting."

Lord Montagu's eyes narrowed at that. Eliza could tell he was upset with her for raising the issue of Barnsley again. She hated to upset her father, but she couldn't risk the police not considering Barnsley as a suspect. Not when the alternative was one of them potentially winding up in prison.

"Yes, you've mentioned that," Abernathy replied. "Did anyone else leave the party?"

"Melville, if memory serves, you took a bit of a jaunt, yes?" Jacob said. This revelation startled Eliza. She had no idea Melville had also stepped away from the party.

"Why yes, Old Chap, I do believe I did step away for a moment. Thank you for the reminder. I had completely forgotten."

Eliza saw the Inspector's eyes light up at this, and her heartbeat quickened. The last thing she wanted was Melville getting caught in one of the man's traps.

"And what exactly did you step away for?"

"That's a great question, Inspector," Melville said. "But it has a rather dull answer, I'm afraid. Without Eliza here to keep things interesting, the evening turned into a bit of a bore. I slipped off to the wine cellar to have a nip of whiskey. The wine they served with dinner was simply not strong enough to make the conversation seem compelling."

Great Aunt Martha inhaled sharply, clearly annoyed by Melville's rudeness. Eliza could not help but note the double standard. Had she said something as brash as the answer Melville had just uttered, there was no universe where Great Aunt Martha would have let it slide with just a sigh of disapproval. There would have been a diatribe the likes of which even Shakespeare himself could not have penned.

"Interesting. I've always had a fondness for a good Scottish whisky. Tell me, what kind was it?"

"An Old Royal Brackla Fine Whiskey. 1812."

Inspector Abernathy's eyes widened at this—as did Lord Montagu's. Had they not been surrounded by law enforcement, Eliza suspected Inspector Abernathy would have soon had a second murder to investigate.

"Sorry, father," Melville said.

Eliza had never seen her father work harder to maintain his composure. Not even that summer when she had rescued a skunk from a nearby pelt farm and snuck it into Thistlewood House. Her father had found it one morning before breakfast, and it got startled and sprayed him. Six tomato baths weren't enough to take out the smell, and to this day, Eliza swore that if you got close enough to the curtains that he'd been standing beside, you could still catch a whiff of it.

But there was something about Melville's admission that she found even more jarring: She was absolutely certain it was a lie.

Eliza knew the precise bottle Melville was referring to. It was her father's most expensive Scottish whiskey, the prize jewel of his collection—which was why, when Ollie and Eliza had stumbled down to the cellar one night, two teenagers tipsy on moonlight and sherry, and drunk half the bottle without thinking, Eliza got up the next morning and filled it with water so no one would notice. She'd also added in a bit of tea to get the color right. It was a convincing fake—one she was sure would be sufficient because she knew her father well enough to know he would never actually crack open the bottle—but there was no way it would pass muster if someone actually drank it.

Eliza was so busy trying to sort out what would have possessed Melville to lie that she completely ceased paying attention to what was happening in the room. It wasn't until Inspector Abernathy called her name for the third time that she even heard a word being said around her.

"Lady Montagu," Abernathy said sharply. "Have I bored you?"

"No, I apologize. It's…been a long day and I got very little sleep last night, as I'm sure you can imagine."

"Of course. I was just saying that I had what I needed from the exercise, and everyone was free to go, back to Thistlewood, but from here on out, I would ask that no one leave the house, even for a walk on the grounds."

"Alright," Eliza said, though she was far from pleased with that directive.

"I was also saying that I hoped you would stay put for a moment. I'd like to speak with you privately. Would that be alright?"

"Certainly," Eliza said, though the thought of staying behind for a private interrogation was absolutely anything other than alright.

Lord Montagu placed his hand gently on Eliza's shoulder as he walked out of the room, and Ollie shot her a glance that would have been comforting were it not for the clear concern in his eyes.

Soon, it was just Eliza, Salisbury, and the Inspector, who sat down across from her, a notebook in hand.

"I just wanted to go over a few things from your statement, if you don't mind."

"Of course."

"You said you spoke with Darlington at dinner, but aside from that and the note you conveniently forgot to mention, you had no other contact with him. Is that correct?"

"Yes."

"That's interesting, Miss Montagu, because the trouble is we have a statement from one of the servants saying they saw you and Lord Darlington talking on the steps outside just before everyone made the transition from dinner to drinks."

"That is interesting," Eliza said. Her head was swirling, and she wanted to buy time to think of a plan, but Abernathy was too fast. Ollie was right. He was so much worse than Salisbury.

"It seems that you've lied to us, Miss Montagu. You can see why that might make us suspicious."

"Yes," Eliza said. "And had I done so intentionally, you would be right to be suspicious, but I did not. That conversation with Darlington was a blip—a few words about my dog on my way inside. The night had been stressful, and I had had a bit to drink. Truthfully, I did not remember the encounter had even occurred until you mentioned it just now."

"Forgive me, Miss, if I find that hard to believe," Inspector Abernathy said.

"You may believe what you like, Darling. Your lack of faith does not make it any less true."

"We spoke with the stable hand," the Constable interjected. "He doesn't remember you. Doesn't remember much of anything, really. Your only hope for an alibi was drunk as a skunk. It's not looking good for you, Miss Montagu. Not looking good at all."

Eliza wanted to knock the satisfied sneer right off his face, but instead, she simply smiled and said, "Is that all?"

"For now," the Inspector replied.

"Good," Eliza said as she got up and began to exit the marquee. "Have a good day, gentlemen."

With that, Eliza left the marquee and began walking across the estate. She knew she should have been thinking more about her own predicament, but in this moment, all she could think about was Melville. Why would he lie? And where was he really during that dinner?

And then, suddenly, Eliza was hit with a realization that made her blood run cold. She couldn't afford to waste another second. She had to get to Melville.

CHAPTER TWENTY TWO

Eliza's head was spinning as she rushed through the grand marble foyer and towards the East Wing. She knew she had to talk to Melville, but for the first time in the history of her relationship with him, she wasn't sure what to say. Things had always been so easy between them. There were times she was convinced he was the only one in the family who understood her.

Cedric had always been kind to Eliza, and she adored Mercy, but Melville—Melville was a kindred spirit. He wasn't made for the aristocracy either, and he found the formalities, traditions, and trivialities every bit as absurd as Eliza did. As much heat as Eliza had taken for her unorthodox views and activism, she would have taken far more were it not for Melville. He was a pleasant distraction and a partner in crime. But this time, Eliza feared he had gone too far, and while she knew that she must confront him about it, she hadn't the slightest idea how.

By the time she arrived at his room, she was no closer to a plan than when she had left the marquee, which made it slightly less vexing when she discovered he wasn't there. While it meant finding him would be harder, it also meant that she would have more time to decide on an approach.

Eliza took stock of where they were in the day and tried to think about what Melville might be doing, which, she quickly realized, was an impossible task because Melville loathed schedules and was almost never where he was supposed to be. And that's when it hit her—Melville had lied to the Inspector. He had said he was somewhere he obviously wasn't, and now, he would need to cover his tracks. All it would take was someone checking on that bottle to know he was lying, and while Melville might be a bit irresponsible and more than a bit of a playboy, he certainly wasn't a fool. He would know he had to cover his tracks, and he would also know time was of the essence.

He was in the cellar. Eliza was sure of it.

Eliza hurried down the back staircase. With each step, the air got cooler until it felt as though the chill was going to settle directly into her bones. Normally, she liked the feeling of heading into the cellar. It felt like she was embarking on some grand adventure. But today, it felt different. Sinister, somehow.

There were no gaslights in the cellar, so Eliza had grabbed a lantern before heading down the staircase. It illuminated little more than the step in front of her and cast a series of shadows on the walls, further adding to the sinister effect.

As she reached the bottom of the stairs, the room opened up before her, expanding into a cavern. The ceiling was made of thick, packed dirt, and the walls were lined with hundreds of cases of wine and whiskey. Ahead, she could hear the clinking of glass.

Melville.

Eliza steadied herself as she headed towards the sound of the glass. She held up her lantern and squinted her eyes as Melville's shadow began to take shape. He was so focused on what he was doing that he didn't hear her approaching until she was nearly upon him, and when he finally saw her, he was so startled, he dropped the bottle he was holding.

"Blimey, Eliza! You scared me!"

"I can see that."

"What are you doing here?"

"I could ask you the same thing."

Melville looked at Eliza quizzically.

"Is everything alright?"

"No. I know, Mel."

"Know what?"

"I know."

Eliza was hoping that, if she just kept telling him she knew, she wouldn't have to come out and accuse him, but that plan clearly did not seem to be working. So, she decided to try and ease him into a confession.

"I know you lied about the whiskey."

"I didn't—"

"Don't, Mel. Don't lie to me."

Melville's face fell, and his eyes focused on his shoes. He couldn't bring himself to look at Eliza, and it broke her heart. Mel had made a lot of questionable choices in his lifetime, but she'd never seen him ashamed.

"I know you didn't drink the whiskey, Mel," she said again. "And I know why. I know where you were."

"You do?" he said, his eyes fluttering back up to Eliza. "How?"

"That's not important. What is important is that I know. And this is bad, Mel. Mother and Father will be beside themselves."

"I know."

"You have to do the right thing here, Mel. You have to come clean and own up to your responsibilities."

"I know."

"I just don't understand how this happened. You've always had a bit of a reputation, but—"

"I know! I just—I got in too deep. I thought I had it under control, but I had a really bad hand, and—"

"It hardly seems fair to blame it on your hand, Mel."

"But if I had just gotten that queen of spades, none of this would have happened!"

Eliza stared at him for a moment. For the life of her, she couldn't make sense of what he was saying.

"What are you talking about?"

"The gambling debt," Mel said, clearly confused.

"What gambling debt?"

"You said you knew!"

"I did—just not about that."

"What then!"

"The baby!"

Eliza had never seen anyone look more shell-shocked than Mel did in that moment—and she had volunteered in a hospital during the war.

"I...I'm not, I didn't—the what?" he stammered.

"The baby. I know all about the baby and Molly and the affair, Mel. There's no sense in hiding it."

"I...I don't even know anyone named Molly."

"Of course you do. She's one of the maids."

"I did not have an affair with the maid."

"Of course you did."

"I think I would know, Eliza," Mel said with a laugh.

"So, you didn't..."

"I did not. Sorry, Old Girl, but you're going to have to wait a little longer to become an aunt. I remain an avowed bachelor. And Lord knows Cedric is too busy burying his face in ledgers to bury his face in anything else."

"Melville!" Eliza exclaimed, though, in truth she wasn't outraged. It was nice to see him joking again, and Eliza felt deeply relieved to find out that he wasn't the father of Molly's baby. For a moment, she felt genuinely relaxed—or at least she did until she realized this meant she no longer had any idea why he left the party.

"So, if you didn't sneak off to see Molly, why did you leave?"

"Because of that bad hand. I've run up some gambling debts, Liza. Some big ones."

"How bad is it?"

"It's bad. Initially, I thought I could pay them off with watches and cufflinks, but it wasn't enough, so I took money from the business to give them. I told them I'd bring it to them next week, but they got tired of waiting. They came all the way out here and sent one of the servants to come get me. That's why I left the party. They said they'd come in and demand the money in the middle of dinner if I didn't. So, I got the money I took and—"

"The money you stole," Eliza interrupted. She couldn't believe what she was hearing. She wasn't sure she'd ever been so angry.

"I was going to put it back before anyone noticed, but—"

"How much," Eliza demanded.

"Too much."

Eliza stared at Melville. Her pulse was pounding in her ears, and she could feel her cheeks flushing with rage. Eliza had always been good at controlling her temper, but now...now, she knew she needed to get out of here before she said something she would later regret.

"I can't even look at you right now," Eliza said, taking her lantern and whipping back around towards the stairs.

"Eliza! Eliza, wait!"

"Melville, if you know what's good for you, you'd best not follow me," she said as she stormed up the stairs and back into the main house.

"Good heavens, Eliza, watch your feet," Great Aunt Martha exclaimed as she spotted Eliza storming through the lobby. "You are a lady. You must walk like one. We can't have you clomping through the house like a horse."

Eliza did not even bother answering. She just kept walking.

Her plan had been to go to the conservancy. Ideally, she would have gone to wander the grounds, but with the Inspector's decree, this was the closest she could get. But Thistlewood had other plans. As she walked past her parents' bedroom, she was surprised to hear three distinct voices. She was more surprised to hear the repeated use of her name.

As angry as she was, she couldn't resist the urge to know what they were saying. The presence of someone else in her parents' room was just too strange not to investigate.

Once again, Eliza found herself pressing her ear against a door in hopes of better hearing the words being spoken on the other side.

This is ridiculous, she thought to herself. *You're an artist, not a character in an Agatha Christie novel!*

Still, she pressed her ear against the door harder, straining to hear what was being said on the other side. It took a moment, but eventually she was able to identify the subject of the conversation. And for the second time today, she found herself filled with unexpected fury.

"I cannot believe you're trying to marry me off!" she said as she threw open the door.

"Eliza!" her father exclaimed, clearly surprised and, Eliza thought, also a bit ashamed.

"A man is dead, we are all under suspicion of murder, but yet, somehow, my marital status is still the primary area of concern."

"Calm down, Eliza," her mother said. "Why must you always make things so dramatic?"

"We are literally living in a murder mystery, mother. If ever there was a time for dramatic, it's now."

"Eliza, please, let us explain," her father said, but Eliza didn't want to hear it. There was nothing he could say right now that would make this better.

Wordlessly, she turned around to leave.

"Eliza! Eliza, please!" he called after her, but Eliza did not stop. She had never regretted anything more than she regretted coming back to Thistlewood.

She didn't care what the Inspector said. She didn't care if it made her look suspicious. She had to get out of here, and she had to get out of here now.

CHAPTER TWENTY THREE

Eliza marched through the halls of Thistlewood House, her footsteps echoing furiously across the marble floor. The servants were starting to stare, and she knew this would be cause for an endless lecture on the way a Lady should behave should she happen to catch the eye of Great Aunt Martha, but in this exact moment, she could not have cared less. She was filled with righteous anger, and for once in her life, she didn't care who knew it.

"Are you alright, Lady Montagu?" Parkins asked as she stormed past the spiral staircase, his face a mix of surprise and concern.

"Far from it," Eliza said as she continued her quest for the exit. "Quite far."

She did not slow down until she reached the back door. She knew the Inspector's rule, but she didn't care about that either. She didn't care if it made her look suspicious. At the moment, she didn't even care if he put a warrant out for her arrest. She had to get out of Thistlewood, and she had to get out of there now.

It wasn't until she clasped her hand around the burnished bronze doorknob that would allow her to escape out onto the estate that her heartrate finally began to slow and she started to feel as though she could breathe again. She was seconds away from an escape, and she could not have been more desperate for it. She needed the thick sound of hushed gossip to be replaced by the rich melody of birdsongs. She needed the stale, suffocating indoor air to be replaced by the feeling of a warm breeze on her face. She needed to get out of Thistlewood House and be somewhere—anywhere—else.

As Eliza began to pull the door open, she found herself breathing a sigh of relief. But that relief was quickly replaced by frustration as a large hand reached over her and pushed the door closed.

She didn't even have to turn around to see who it was. She would have recognized those cufflinks anywhere. She'd always found them terribly ostentatious, but he loved them, and she loved him, so she'd let it slide.

"Cedric, now is not the time," Eliza said firmly.

"Be reasonable, Eliza."

Eliza turned to face him. *What an utterly useless piece of advice,* she thought. *When was the last time anything great was ever achieved by being reasonable?*

"I appreciate you looking out for me, brother, but my mind is made up."

"The Inspector will think this is proof of your guilt"

"He already thinks I'm guilty. Might as well get some fresh air out of the deal."

"He could arrest you, Liza."

Eliza was about to say something smart, but something stopped her. She wasn't sure if it was the expression on his face—one that reminded her of every lost puppy she had ever rescued—or the fact that he called her Liza, which he had often done when she was a child, but whatever the case, she felt compelled to take him seriously.

"Please, don't go," he pleaded. "You won't get far, and it will only make things worse."

Much as she hated to admit it, she knew that Cedric was right. The Inspector had been adamant that they were not to leave the house. Doing so could be grounds for arrest, and she couldn't very well investigate the murder if she was sitting in prison.

"Come to dinner with me," he continued. "You always feel better after you've eaten. And I hear Rene is making that chicken dish you like."

"Coq au vin?" Eliza asked.

That sneaky devil, Eliza thought. *He knows full well that I can't turn down a chance at a good coq au vin.*

"Guess you'll have to come see," Cedric said with a grin before taking a puff of his pipe. He had Eliza, and he knew it.

"Okay," she said with a slight smile. "But if it's not accompanied by crème brûlée for dessert, I shall leave Thistlewood at once and never return."

Cedric laughed.

"I should expect nothing less, sister," he said, offering her his elbow, which she happily took.

***

Given the events of the previous evening, no one had any interest in eating in the marquee, so they had arranged to have dinner in one of Thistlewood's other dining rooms. While it was not quite as festive as the marquee, it was far from lacking in grandeur.

The walls were lined with thick, hand-cut, oak panels, and a candelabra hung from the beamed ceiling. Rich, intricate rugs covered a large-stone floor, and a dining room table big enough for twenty sat in the center of the room, topped with a meticulously hand-embroidered white tablecloth. Bone china place settings were set next to flawlessly folded silk napkins, and stunning flowers from the garden served as the perfect centerpieces.

It was, Eliza thought, *a far better room than their company deserved.*

Cedric escorted Eliza to a seat towards the head of the table, as far away from Lady Darlington and their parents as possible. As he pulled out her chair, Eliza could feel Lady Darlington's eyes on her. Had it been possible to shoot fire from her gaze, Eliza was certain she would have been burned to a crisp.

"I was not aware she was coming," Lady Darlington said pointedly.

"Mother—" Jacob began.

"I cannot possibly be expected to sit here and share a meal with my son's murderer!"

Eliza started to say something, but she decided against it. No sense in retreading the same ground. Lady Darlington was never going to be convinced of Eliza's innocence, or, at the very least, she was not going to budge until presented with the real killer. Eliza knew her energy would be far better spent solving that mystery than trying to win over a curmudgeonly old bat.

Ollie, however, was less inclined to let the slander slide.

"Miss Montagu is a member of the family, Lady Darlington. Her presence here is both welcome and expected. If you don't like it, I'm sure we could arrange to have you set with the servants for the evening. We all know how desperately fond your family is of them."

Eliza couldn't help smiling, both at Oliver's wit and his unexpected rise to her rescue. She also couldn't resist the chance at a little banter.

"Oh, Ollie that's awfully kind of you, but it seems terribly unfair to the servants. After all, they've done nothing wrong. Seems cruel to punish them with such miserable company."

"Eliza!" Great Aunt Martha chided.

"Oh, I'm sorry, Great Aunt Martha," Eliza said in a tone that made it very clear she was in no way sorry. "You're right. That is a terrible tone to take with my future mother-in-law. I should be much more polite to the family Mother and Father are trying to force me into."

For as long as Eliza had been alive, she had believed Great Aunt Martha to be in possession of only two facial expressions: boredom and displeasure. Tonight, Eliza was stunned to discover a third: surprise.

"Oh, had you not heard? Now that their first choice has been bumped off, they're trying to offer me to the younger Darlington—because one time of treating me as some sort of bargaining chip simply wasn't enough."

"Eliza…" her father began.

Eliza had always had a soft spot for her father. While they quite often failed to see eye to eye, Eliza knew his most egregious views were a product of his time—and also his marriage to her mother. As such, she had always been inclined to give him the benefit of the doubt and to assume his intentions were good. But she simply could not do that tonight. Not after everything that had happened.

"Where am I wrong, father?" she demanded. "Tell me one part of that statement that is incorrect, and I shall recant immediately."

But Lord Montagu couldn't, and he knew it.

Everyone sat silently for a moment, the tension so thick that you could have spread it on one of Rene's award-winning crumpets.

"Two arranged marriages in as many days for Eliza, and not a single suitor for me?" Mercy asked, feigning offense in an effort to lighten the mood. "Can you all see me? Am I invisible? Did I become invisible, and you all just failed to tell me? Because that is really the sort of thing one ought to tell a person."

Eliza couldn't help but laugh, and soon the rest of the table—sans Lady Darlington—was laughing too.

Just as everyone began to relax a bit, the servants arrived with the food. Eliza's mouth watered at the sight of Rene's coq au vin—the smell alone was heaven—which was why Eliza found herself so surprised when no one even so much as lifted a fork. Instead, they just gazed at each other anxiously.

"What is going on?" Eliza asked

"It's just, with the murderer not caught…" Mercy began.

"Oh, you can't be serious," Eliza said.

"It just seems like an unnecessary risk," Melville said.

"You certainly didn't feel that way about the wine," Eliza said, pointing to his glass which was now nearly empty.

"Cedric, you were the one who told me to come to dinner! Surely you're not—"

"I hadn't thought about it before now," he said. "But now that we're here it seems…unwise."

122

"This is absurd."

"Then eat it," Lady Darlington interjected. "But do so from my plate. If you're the murderer, you certainly wouldn't have poisoned your own food, now would you?"

"Willis, would you bring me Lady Darlington's plate, please? I have a point to prove."

Willis brought Eliza Lady Darlington's plate, and Eliza readied her fork dramatically. The whole room stared at her in anxious anticipation.

Eliza took a bite of the coq au vin. The richness of the red wine and lardons partnered perfectly with the earthy mushrooms, and the chicken was braised so beautifully it was literally falling off the bone. Rene had outdone himself.

Eliza closed her eyes for a moment, savoring the depth of flavor before opening them to find every eye in the room fixated on her.

She opened her mouth as though to say something, but instead, she began to cough. It was a slight cough at first, but then it began to build, thundering through her body until her face began to redden and her eyes started to water.

"She's—she's been poisoned!" Lady Darlington sputtered. "Someone poisoned her too! I was right! They planned to kill me! They—"

"Eliza? Eliza are you alright?" Cedric asked.

But Eliza did not answer. She just continued to cough.

CHAPTER TWENTY FOUR

"Eliza!" Cedric said again, true concern creeping into his face now. He slapped Eliza on the back, hard, until a piece of chicken came flying out of her mouth and whizzed across the table.

"Are you alright?" Cedric asked her as the rest of the table stared on in horror. The truth was that Eliza was more than a little rattled, but she wasn't about to let them know that.

"Yes, quite alright, Old Chap," she said with a smile. "But I must say, you should try the food. The chicken is simply to die for."

Everyone stared at her for a moment, completely unsure how to respond, until Mercy began to laugh. It was just a quite giggle at first, but it built until she was laughing so hard that she had tears in her eyes.

As is often the case, the laughter was contagious, and soon everyone but the Darlingtons were caught up in it.

"I suppose we are being a bit ridiculous," Mercy said, once she had begun to recover herself.

"Quite," Eliza said. "Even if someone were reckless enough to commit another murder with both the Constable and the Inspector around, they would hardly be foolish enough to do it again in precisely the same way. Rene is watching over that food like a hawk. It would be impossible to embark on such a task without getting caught."

"It seems as though you've given this a great deal of thought," Lady Darlington said. "Seems the sort of thing a murderer would do."

"Oh, Lady Darlington, please do shut up," Great Aunt Martha said, in a moment that shocked and delighted Eliza to her core.

"Well, I never," Lady Darlington huffed. "I will not be spoken to this way."

With that, she stood up and began storming out of the room.

"Come along, Jacob," she said as she walked towards the door.

But Jacob didn't budge.

"Actually, Mother, I think I'll stay. I've heard the coq au vin is simply to die for."

"Well played, Old Chap. Well played," Eliza said with a grin.

Eliza was surprised by Jacob. If they'd met under different circumstances, she might have even liked him. In another lifetime or another universe, they could have even been a good match, but not like this. How could her parents do this? After everything that had happened, why would they still be pushing this—especially now when Darlington's body was barely even cold?

And why the sudden rush to marry her off? Certainly, Mother and Great Aunt Martha had long wanted to see her partnered, and her stubborn independence had been a bit of a stone in their shoe, but prior to this week, they had dealt with it largely through elaborate sighs and subtle digs. This sudden shift wreaked of desperation, and Eliza didn't understand it.

Truth be told, she didn't feel like she understood much of anything right now. She did not understand her parents' actions. She did not understand how Melville could have been so selfish and irresponsible. She did not understand what had happened to Darlington—and perhaps that was the worst of all. Because if she could not figure that out, and soon, the consequences could be truly dire.

**

Eliza lay in bed, watching the curtains dance slightly in the night breeze. Scout was snuggled up beside her, and Eliza absentmindedly scratched behind his ear as he snored slightly.

It was getting late, and she knew she should sleep, but she couldn't. She just kept turning questions over and over in her mind.

What were her parents hiding, and did that have anything to do with why Barnsley was there?

Why was Barnsley there?

And what about Molly? If Melville wasn't the father of her baby, who was?

She needed to clear her head—to think—but she couldn't do that here. She needed to feel grass beneath her feet and breathe fresh air bathed in moonlight. As much as she loved Thistlewood, she needed to get out of this house.

She knew she was taking a risk. After all, the Inspector had expressly forbidden them from even so much as stepping foot outside. But she also knew for a fact that the Inspector had come down with a headache and turned in early as a result, so it wasn't like she was going to bump into him on her way out. And what he didn't know wouldn't hurt him.

She slipped out of bed as quietly as she could in an effort to not disturb Scout, but he woke up the moment her feet hit the floor. He was at the door even before she was, crying quietly in hopes of joining her for her nighttime excursion.

"Oh, alright. Come along, you little beggar."

Eliza grabbed the leash off her nightstand and slipped it around his neck. His tail wagged furiously, and if Eliza didn't know any better, she would have sworn she saw him smile.

She opened the door quietly and began padding down the hallway, Scout at her side. Under the cloak of darkness, Eliza slipped through the house and to the backdoor. She found herself holding her breath as she turned the doorknob, anxiously listening for even the slightest hint of footsteps behind her, but no noise ever came. So, she gently pushed open the French Door and stepped outside.

Almost immediately, she felt her muscles begin to relax. Her breath came easier than it had since she'd arrived, and her mind was instantly clearer. Painting had always been the activity that helped Eliza feel most relaxed and at home with herself but walking the grounds of Thistlewood was a close second.

Scout seemed a bit frightened by the darkness, but Eliza was right at home. Using the moon to guide her, she made her way through the hedge maze and snuck into a hidden spot behind the topiaries. When she was a child, Cedric had read Eliza *The Secret Garden*, and Eliza had fallen in love with it—so much so that one year for her birthday, Cedric made her a small secret garden of her own. It had long been her favorite spot on the grounds.

Eliza made her way to the secret entrance and through the tunnel of rhododendron. The night breeze brought the smell of roses, and Eliza couldn't help but smile. But it brought something else too. Something unexpected. It brought a sudden awareness that Eliza was not here alone.

The noise was subtle but unmistakable. Someone was on her hidden swing. Scout could tell too, and he was desperate to investigate. He whined as he tugged on the leash.

"Oh, hush," Eliza said gently. "All in good time."

With that, she slowly began creeping forward, hoping Scout would stay quiet long enough for her to properly assess the situation.

She expected it to be Ollie. He was the only one she'd ever told about this place, and he was far more likely than Cedric to break the rules or fail to follow orders. Cedric would never defy the Inspector, but Ollie might.

As she peered at the swing, however, she was surprised to find neither Cedric nor Ollie. Instead, on the swing, sat Jacob Darlington.

"What are you doing here?" she asked. Her tone was neither harsh nor accusatory, but still, Jacob nearly jumped out of his skin.

"Hell's bells, Eliza! What are you doing here?"

"I asked you first," she said with a grin. She expected to feel more territorial about the place, but there was something about Jacob on that swing that was just so utterly charming that she couldn't be anything other than happy to see him.

"Just needed to clear my head. I know the Inspector said we couldn't, but—"

"What he doesn't know won't hurt him," Eliza offered.

"Yes! Exactly."

Eliza sat down on a nearby bench and stared at Jacob for a moment, trying to decide what else to say. The silence between them was slightly awkward, but there was a strange comfort to it that Eliza had not been expecting.

"I'm sorry about my mother," Jacob said, his eyes fixed firmly on the ground in front of him.

"I'm sorry about my mother," Eliza said gently. She could tell Jacob was upset, and it pleased her to be able to make him smile as she had now.

"I didn't ask them to arrange a marriage."

"I know," Jacob said. He stopped for a moment, pumping his legs lightly so the swing rocked him gently before continuing. "I don't wish to marry you, Eliza. I hope you know that's nothing personal. I think you're wonderful, and—"

"It's okay," Eliza replied. "In truth, I really don't want to marry you either."

Jacob smiled, but underneath the smile, she identified something else. Relief.

"I didn't kill your brother," she offered.

"I did not for one moment think that you did."

"Good."

The silence creeped back in again, but Eliza didn't care. She was too busy staring at the stars, which were on absolutely spectacular display this evening. Eventually, she was pulled back to reality by Scout, who arrived at her feet several minutes later, one of mother's prized peonies in his mouth.

"How did you find this place?" Eliza asked. She wasn't sure what insight that was going to provide, but she nevertheless thought there would be some.

"My brother showed it to me, actually."

"Interesting. How did he find it?

"I'm not sure. Stumbled upon it, I suppose."

Eliza nodded, and the two sat in comfortable silence again—this time with Jacob staring off in the distance and Eliza once again staring off at the stars.

"Do you have any other thoughts on who might have killed your brother?" Eliza asked. She knew that, perhaps, it was an insensitive thing to ask right now, but she couldn't help it. If she was going to solve this case before the Constable arrested the wrong person, she had to get as many answers as she could as quickly as she could.

"I don't really know," Jacob said, but there was something in his tone that told Eliza there was more to that story.

"But you have a suspicion?" she asked.

"I—"

"It's okay," Eliza said. "You can tell me. Whatever it is, I won't judge. I am far more open-minded than the rest of the Montagus."

"That, I knew," Jacob said with a grin. He swung back and forth for a minute, and Eliza had to imagine he was hoping he could swing so hard it would just propel him out of here. But that's not how life works—a thought that must also have occurred to Jacob because he suddenly changed his mind about not sharing his suspicions.

"I hate to admit this," Jacob said. "After all, it's really just rumor and innuendo, and I hate to slander my dead brother's name over something that might not even be true, but…"

"But?" Eliza said, hoping to prod him into providing more information.

"But I've heard that he had a tendency to be…inappropriate with the female staff. Perhaps one of them had a jealous lover, or—"

"Jacob, when did your brother show you this place?"

"The last time we were here. Why?"

"And when was that?" Eliza asked. She was beginning to get excited. She could tell that she was on to something, and she could not wait for Jacob to confirm her suspicions.

"Six or seven weeks ago, probably. Why?"

Because, Eliza thought to herself, *that means there's a very good chance Darlington was the father of Molly's baby. And if that was true, there's a very good chance that it's the reason he's dead.*

CHAPTER TWENTY FIVE

It was nearing nine, far later than Eliza would typically have ever entered the servant's quarters, but she knew this couldn't wait. If Molly was the killer, she needed to know now. She couldn't afford to give Inspector Abernathy and the Constable any more time to formulate a false theory of the crime.

As she walked down the corridor where the servants were housed, she found herself wishing her family had spent the money to install more lights in this side of the house. It was darker here than it was in the areas the family inhabited, and it made it difficult to navigate things in the evening. They could always carry a lantern, of course, but that was cumbersome if you had other things to carry, and it also meant anyone who stayed here had to be able to locate and light their lanterns in the dark. It was a hassle, and Eliza hated seeing all of the little ways in which her family had chosen to make their lives easier while failing to extend those same small conveniences to the servants.

With Scout by her side, Eliza made her way to Molly's room. She had convinced Rene to tell her its location by pretending she wanted to bring the maid something to settle her stomach. Rene had given her some ginger biscuits, which she carried with her now. She felt badly about the ruse, but the girl would likely benefit from the biscuits regardless. And ascertaining her whereabouts was of the utmost importance, so Eliza tried hard not to feel guilty about the decision to secure that information by whatever means necessary.

Eliza stopped outside of room thirteen and knocked on the door gently. When at least thirty seconds had passed by without response, she knocked again.

Still nothing.

"Molly," she whispered, but there was no reply. She said her name again, slightly louder this time, and when she still did not get a response, she quietly began trying to turn the doorknob. She was pleased to find it unlocked.

Eliza slipped quickly into Molly's bedchamber. She was once again struck by how bare and utterly devoid of comfort the servant's rooms were. She could not imagine the panic Molly must have felt upon realizing she was pregnant. The shame and social stigma of being an unwed mother was already more weight than anyone should have to carry. And this? Well, this was certainly no place to raise a child.

Scout began tugging on the leash, so Eliza let it fall.

"Go ahead, boy," she said. "Take a look around. And be sure to let me know if you uncover anything interesting."

If Eliza didn't know any better, she would swear that the hound understood her, as he immediately began wandering around the room, aggressively sniffing everything in sight.

As Scout scoured the floor, Eliza began exploring the higher surfaces. There was depressingly little to look through. Molly clearly had almost nothing to her name, which made Eliza feel even worse about looking through what little she did have.

Regardless, it must be done, Eliza thought as she gingerly worked her way through every article of clothing Molly owned. As she moved through the uniforms, undergarments, and outfits for a rare venture outside of Thistlewood, Eliza was struck by just how utilitarian everything was.

Eliza's own wardrobe was filled with bits and bobbles. She had outfits for dinners and galas, for marches and galleries. She had jewelry and hair pins, and a litany of things she owned simply because the liked them. But Molly, Eliza couldn't imagine there was a single item she'd purchased for love or for fun. Everything here was plain and fit for purpose, and there was something about that that struck Eliza as terribly sad.

I must get a gift for the servants this Christmas, she thought. Something festive and fun that they would never allow themselves otherwise.

Eliza was just about to begin brainstorming potential Christmas presents when Scout jolted her out of her thoughts and back to the task at hand. He was standing by Molly's bed, growling ferociously and pawing at the bedframe.

Scout was seated next to the bottom right corner of Molly's bed, so naturally, that was where Eliza began investigating. It only took a moment for her to find the source of Scout's upset, and when she did, her blood ran cold.

There, at the foot of the bed, between the mattress and the bedframe, was what looked like a small parcel. A white handkerchief had been wrapped around a small, black bottle, and as Eliza peeled back the handkerchief, a small skull and crossbones icon revealed itself.

Hidden in Molly's room was a bottle of poison—no doubt the same poison used to kill Lord Darlington. It broke Eliza's heart to admit it, but faced with such irrefutable evidence, she had no choice but to believe that her hunch had been correct: Lord Darlington fathered Molly's baby, and she'd killed him for it.

The poor girl, Eliza thought. *She must have been so desperate.*

Still, no matter how desperate she may have been, it hardly excused cold-blooded murder. As much as she empathized with her, Eliza knew Molly had to pay for her crimes. She needed to bring this to Inspector Abernathy, and she needed to do so immediately.

But before she could even turn around, Eliza heard a noise that caused her stomach to lurch into her throat. The door she had carefully closed behind her was swinging open. Molly was back.

"What—what are you doing here?" Molly asked. Eliza couldn't help but notice that she did not look well at all. If she had to guess, she would assume Molly had stepped out of the room to be sick.

"I—I came to bring you these," Eliza stammered, uncomfortable with the lie but nevertheless thankful for the cover. "They're ginger biscuits. Rene made them. I asked him for something to help settle your stomach."

"Oh, thank you miss. It's awful kind of you."

Molly took the biscuits eagerly and bit into one. As she did, her eyes closed, and she inhaled deeply. Her face was the very portrait of gratitude, and Eliza could not possibly have felt more guilty.

"Well, I'd best be going," she said, making her way towards the door. "But I hope you're feeling much better soon."

"Thank you," Molly said, taking another bite of the biscuit.

"Lady Eliza?" Molly said just as Eliza's hand closed around the doorknob.

"Yes, Molly?"

"I don't mean to be nosy or nothin', but what's that in your other hand there?"

Molly pointed at the little bottle of poison in Eliza's left hand, and immediately, Eliza's heart sank. She'd been hoping to escape without a confrontation, but there was no hope of that now.

"I know about Darlington," Eliza said softly.

"What about 'im miss?"

"I've heard all about his behavior with the servants, and I find it abhorrent. A woman should never have to endure unsolicited advances from anyone, but especially not some entitled dullard who thinks that,

131

by nature of his title, he should be able to just take whatever he wants from any woman he wants. It's inexcusable."

Molly nodded quietly, though Eliza was surprised to find that she seemed a bit confused. She thought what she was saying was clear, but perhaps she needed to be more direct.

"I'm so sorry for what he did to you, Molly. You have every right to be angry. Furious even. And Darlington deserved to be punished for what he did. But you cannot simply take the law into your own hands like this."

"I...I'm sorry, I...Forgive me, Miss, but I don't understand what you're on about," Molly said. "Lord Darlington didn't do nothing to me."

"I would hardly call fathering your child against your will nothing."

"He didn't—what? No! I didn't even know Lord Darlington. I—"

"I understand it can be painful to talk about these things—" Eliza began.

"It's not that it's painful, Miss. It's that it isn't true."

"Which part?"

"All of it. Lord Darlington wasn't the father of my baby, and I didn't have nothin' to do with his murder."

"If Lord Darlington wasn't the father, who is then?"

"I told you, Lady, I can't say. It would ruin him."

"Okay, let's try a different route then. If Lord Darlington wasn't the father, what are you doing with this?"

Eliza held up the little bottle of poison then, and what little color remained in the girl's face drained completely. She looked to Eliza like a frightened animal. And Eliza knew from experience that frightened animals were not to be trifled with.

For the first time, Eliza realized that she shouldn't have just been worried about trying to escape Molly's room without a confrontation. She should have been worried about trying to get out of Molly's room alive.

CHAPTER TWENTY SIX

"I...I've never seen that before," Molly stammered, staring wide-eyed and terrified at the bottle in Eliza's hand.

"Molly—"

"No, I...I didn't do this, you hear me? I didn't do this!"

"Molly, please. Compose yourself. This stress can't be good for the baby."

"And prison will be?!" Molly exclaimed, her voice getting louder and more hysterical with each passing moment.

"You can't pin this on me, Miss! You can't!"

"I'm not pinning anything—"

"I've never seen that bottle before. Never! You 'ear me? For all I know, you planted it! Everyone said you killed Darlington, and I didn't believe them, but now—"

"Molly, please," Eliza begged. Molly was screaming and crying now, and Eliza was becoming genuinely concerned, not just for her own safety, but for that of Molly and her unborn child.

"I won't let you do this! I won't!" Molly screamed.

Suddenly, there was a knock at the door.

"Everything okay in there?"

Before Eliza could answer, Molly screamed again. "I didn't do this! You can't...you can't..."

As Inspector Abernathy opened the door behind them, Molly dissolved into a fit of tears.

"What's all this then?" He asked, as he surveyed the scene. "Is anyone hurt?"

"No," Eliza replied, as calmy as she could. "But as you can see, she's quite upset."

"And why is that?"

"Because she's the one who killed Lord Darlington," Eliza said. "And now she's been found out."

A small group of servants had gathered outside the hallway—no doubt one of them had summoned Inspector Abernathy—and they gasped at the revelation. Eliza expected Molly to object, but she simply sat on the bed and sobbed.

"That's a serious accusation," Inspector Abernathy said. "What makes you so certain it was her?"

"Lord Darlington had a reputation for making overtures with the servants. His own brother told me as much this evening. Molly here is pregnant—"

Again, there was a gasp from the group behind her, but Eliza paid them no mind.

"She did not tell me his name," Eliza continued, "but she said he would be ruined by the revelation and intimated that he was above her class. Lord Darlington certainly fits that bill, and he was last here between six and seven weeks ago—right at the time of conception."

"That certainly gives her motive, but it is hardly proof of anything," Inspector Abernathy said.

"I know, which is why I came to her room tonight. I was hoping to find something that would tell me one way or the other if Molly was the killer. And find it I did."

With that, Eliza held up the little bottle of poison, prompting whispers of "what is that" and "let me see" from the crowd behind her.

"I'll need to get a look at that," Inspector Abernathy said.

"Of course," Eliza said as she handed the little bottle to him.

"You said her name is…"

"Molly," Eliza offered.

"Molly," Inspector Abernathy said gently, kneeling down in front of her. "Molly, I think we need to talk."

***

Eliza stood on the marble steps outside Thistlewood House, watching as Molly was carted off by the Constable. Though she had never admitted to the murder, both the Inspector and Salisbury had insisted that the fact that she would not reveal the father, combined with the fact that the poison was found in her room and one of the other servants confirmed having seen Darlington make advances towards her on his previous visit, was more than enough to secure a conviction.

Though it was nearing ten o'clock and the fierce cloak of darkness brought about by the hour made it difficult to see, the whole family, as well as Jacob, the Fairfaxes, and many of the servants, had gathered outside to watch Molly's exit. Gossip always seemed to seep through the house like water, so Eliza wasn't surprised that word had gotten out so quickly—even with the late hour.

134

The Constable pulled out of the driveway, kicking up a cloud of dust that Eliza could not quite see in the inky blackness but was nevertheless certain was there. Everyone stood silently for a moment and then, with Molly gone and the drama finally over, began to head back inside one-by-one until there was no one left but Eliza and Ollie.

"Tough night," he said.

"Very," she agreed.

"I'm sorry. I know you didn't want it to be her."

"You are certainly correct about that," Eliza said with a sigh.

"At least it wasn't one of the family," he offered. "And at least you don't have to worry about them having gotten the wrong man. I mean, for heaven's sake, Liza, you caught her red-handed. The poison was literally in her room."

"I know...but that's what's troubling me. If she murdered Darlington, why would she keep the poison?"

"She wasn't in her right mind, Liza. Clearly. She killed someone."

"It's just too tidy. What sort of murderer hangs on to a smoking gun like that? And why refuse to name the father? I understand doing it initially, but why now? She was already implicated in his murder, and he was already dead? Why not just admit he was the father unless I got it wrong? Unless it wasn't him?"

"Oh, Eliza," Oliver said with a sigh. "You never did know how to leave well enough alone."

"That's not fair."

"It is though," he insisted. "This is resolved, Eliza. You found the murderer. You cleared your family's name. Accept the win, Darling."

Eliza was unsure what to say. There was something in his words that hurt her, but she wasn't sure if it was because they felt so paternal, which she hated, or if it was because they were right.

"I'm going to call it a night and turn in," Ollie said. "I would encourage you to do the same. I suspect it will be an early morning."

With that, Oliver headed back into the house. Eliza knew he was right—it was certain to be an early morning. With the requirement to stay at Thistlewood finally lifted, she imagined the Darlingtons and the Fairfaxes would all be on their way first thing in the morning, which meant everyone would be up bright and early to deal with the hustle and bustle of that. But Eliza couldn't bring herself to go to bed, not when so many questions were still needling her.

Most of the house would have been asleep by now, but there was one night owl Eliza knew she could always count on at this late hour: Rene.

"Come along, Scout," she said, summoning the dog and then heading towards the kitchen. She did not even have to open the door to know what delectable treat Rene was working on at the moment. The smell greeted her the moment she entered the corridor that led to the kitchen. Chelsea buns. Her favorite.

"That smells divine, Rene," Eliza said as soon as she spotted him.

"Thank you, love. Care to help?"

Eliza nodded and joined him behind the counter. As he finished rolling out the yeast dough, Eliza grabbed the spice mixture and softened butter he had left sitting out nearby.

"You're up awfully late," Rene said as Eliza began spreading the butter over the dough with a pastry brush. "Couldn't sleep?"

"Something like that. I assume you heard about Molly?"

"I did. Terrible thing," Rene said sadly. "Just terrible."

Having spread the butter across the dough, Eliza began to sprinkle on the spice mixture, Scout whimpering hungrily at her feet. Reluctantly, Rene tossed him a small bit of crust from a nearby bread loaf, which he devoured eagerly.

"Careful!" Rene cautioned. "It must be even."

Eliza slowed down, making sure to be as deliberate as possible with her spice distribution.

"Better. Much better," Rene said, as he placed two small bowls beside her. "Next will be the sultanas and the currents."

Eliza nodded and began sprinkling both over the dough, making sure they were scattered in such a way that you would get at least one of each with every bite. Eliza loved the focused work baking required. It was a wonderful way to quiet the mind. For a minute, she didn't even think about Molly, but as Rene stepped in to begin the more complicated process of rolling and cutting the buns, it all came rushing back.

"I just don't understand. If Molly was the murderer, why wouldn't she just admit that Darlington was the father?"

"Perhaps because he wasn't."

"What do you mean?"

"Think about it. The only reason for Molly to keep quiet at this stage is if she was protecting someone else. And if the father was Darlington, there was certainly no need for that. He was already dead."

"So, you think someone else was the father of her baby?"

"I'm all but certain," Rene said.

"What makes you so sure?"

"I saw them together."

"What? Why didn't you say something sooner!"

"It wasn't my place. But now…"

"Who is it, Rene? You can tell me. Please. For Molly's sake."

Rene was not terribly inclined to betray Molly's confidence, but Eliza was right; it was time. And Rene knew he could trust her, so he did as she asked and told her who the father of Molly's baby was.

And as soon as he did, Eliza desperately wished that he hadn't.

CHAPTER TWENTY SEVEN

"Cedric Thomas Montagu! Cedric Thomas Montagu you open this door this instant!"

Eliza banged on her brother's door as she spoke—loud enough that it echoed down the hallway. Normally, she would have been more discreet, more concerned about the prospect of inadvertently waking people up. But not tonight.

"I mean it, Cedric! You open this door!"

"Bloody hell, Eliza," Cedric said as he pulled the door open, "what has gotten into you? Are you trying to wake the whole house?"

Eliza burst into Cedric's room, and he closed the door behind her. He stared at her, confused, and Eliza was immediately drawn to his eyes. They were red and bleary, though from sleep, drink, tears, or some combination of the three she could not say.

"Tell me it's not true," Eliza said.

"You've got to slow down, Old Girl. I'm at least ten steps behind," Cedric replied, taking a seat on the bed.

"Tell me I'm wrong."

"About what?"

"Tell me you're not the father of that poor girl's baby."

"Eliza—"

"Tell me it's not true! Tell me I'm wrong, Cedric. Tell me there's been some misunderstanding or confusion or…"

"I can't," Cedric said softly.

Eliza immediately stopped pacing and stared at him before sinking into an armchair across from his bed and next to the fireplace.

"Bloody hell, Cedric."

"I know."

"I can't believe you. I know you and I haven't always seen eye to eye, but I thought you were still one of the good ones. Better than this, certainly. To take advantage of that poor girl like that—"

"I didn't—I mean, it wasn't—"

"Wasn't what?" Eliza demanded. She was tired of waiting, though she was far from convinced that there was anything he could say that would make things better anyway.

"I loved her, Liza. I still love her. I'm in love with Molly."

Eliza stared at Cedric for a moment, her eyes eerily wide and unblinking. She was perhaps even more stunned by this than the realization that he was the father. She could scarcely believe her brother had ever even spoken to a maid, much less gotten to know one well enough to profess love for her.

Eliza was starting to feel like she didn't know her brother at all.

"She never told me," Cedric said. "I had no idea she was pregnant until the Inspector explained everything to us tonight. I think she may have tried to—that night, during the dinner at the marquee. But, I was distracted. I wasn't listening. I..."

"Would it have mattered?" Eliza said finally.

"What?"

"If you had known, would you have done things differently? Would you have married her? Raised the baby with her?"

"Eliza..."

"Would you? Tell me Cedric. Would you have stood by the woman you loved, or would you have just left her to handle this crisis on her own?"

"It's not that simple, Eliza, and you know it. I am the eldest. There are certain expectations. We can't all just run off to London and live in a fantasy."

"I hardly think you're in a position to be judging anyone's life choices right now, Darling," Eliza said, her eyes narrowing into a glare.

"I'm sorry. Why don't we both just take a breath."

"I don't need a breath, Cedric. I need a brother who is not a spineless coward!"

Cedric opened his mouth to say something but seemed to think better of it. Eliza, on the other hand, was in no mood to stay quiet.

"The fact that you wouldn't have married her is shameful enough, but my God, man—to just let her take the fall like that. To see her hauled away to prison when you had information that could have saved her—"

"I know," Cedric said, tears welling up in his eyes. Eliza and Cedric had always been close, but she had never, ever seen him cry. It was almost enough to make her feel sorry for him. Not quite, but almost.

"You're right. I'm a spineless coward, and I should be ashamed."

"You made a mistake," Eliza said, standing up and walking over to him. "A lot of mistakes."

She sat down on the bed beside him and took his hand. As angry as she was, her heart also broke for him. Cedric had always been such a good brother to her—so kind and present and generous. She had never let their differences come between them before, and she didn't want to start now. As a child, Cedric had always done what he could to keep Eliza on the straight and narrow path. Maybe now it was her turn to try and get him on the right path.

"It's not too late to change things, Cedric. You can still make this right. You can come downstairs with me right now. We can wake up Inspector Abernathy and tell him the truth. It won't fix everything, but it's a start. It will get Molly out of jail. And we can figure the rest out to together, I promise."

Eliza waited for a response, but none came. She stood up and tugged his hand gently. "Come on, I'll go with you. We can do it together."

"I can't, Liza," he said softly. "I'm so sorry, but I can't."

"Of course you can, Cedric. All you have to do is stand up, come with me, and tell the truth. You can do that. I know you can."

"It wouldn't change anything. Maybe if it would then it would be worth it, but it won't. The poison was found in her room."

"But she has no motive!"

"No, she just doesn't have that motive. You said it yourself, Eliza. Darlington was terrible to the servants—terrible enough that you thought it could have been a motive for murder. The Inspector knows that. Add to that the poison you found and the fact that he'd made advances towards her, and it just...me telling them about my relationship with her doesn't change things Eliza. I'm sorry, but it doesn't."

Eliza had long since come to the conclusion that most people were disappointing if you got to know them well enough. Men, especially. But she had never been more disappointed in anyone than she was in Cedric in this moment.

She stared at him in shock, shook her head, and then started for the door.

"Eliza. Eliza, wait!"

Eliza turned back briefly and shook her head.

"I'm sorry, Cedric, but I can't be around you right now," she said, stepping out into the hallway and closing the door behind her.

Much like her brother, Eliza had never been one for tears, so she found herself surprised when they began welling up—clouding her vision and making it even harder to make her way down the dark hallway.

Pull it together, Eliza, she thought. *Crying never fixed anything, and besides, you have a murder to solve.*

The reality was that if Cedric wasn't going to intervene, the only way to free Molly was to find the real killer. The problem was Eliza had absolutely no idea who that might be. But she couldn't let Molly just sit in prison, not when she was innocent. And especially not when Eliza was the one who put her there.

As Eliza rounded the corner and started down an adjacent corridor, she nearly jumped out of her skin as she felt something brush against the side of her leg. It was dark, so it took her a moment to sort out what it was, but when she did, she felt a rush of relief.

"Oh, Scout! What are you doing here?" she said, as she knelt down beside him and scratched the scruff of his neck.

Eliza had left Scout in the kitchen when she went to confront Cedric. Despite Rene's disdain for the idea of having a dog in a space where food was prepared, he had promised to look out for him. Eliza could only assume Scout must have snuck out somehow, and while she knew it couldn't realistically have been the case, as he wagged his tail and gently tried to lick away Eliza's tears, she couldn't help wondering if some part of him hadn't come to find her because he knew she needed comfort.

"That's a good boy," she said, scratching a spot behind his ear he loved so much that his foot instinctively started tapping.

For a brief moment, Eliza forgot all about Cedric and Molly and Lord Darlington and the Inspector. For a brief moment, the only thing on Eliza's mind was Scout—how happy he was and how pleased she was that she'd saved him. But then, suddenly Scout stopped short. His foot no longer tapped with the rhythm of Eliza's fingers, and he stood up, muscles taught, eyes firmly focused on something Eliza could not yet see.

"Is someone there?" she whispered.

Scout didn't need to say anything. His body language made it clear that the answer was yes.

It was late enough that seeing anyone out and about in the house would have been odd. Add that to that the fact that the murderer was still on the loose and it was downright disconcerting. Eliza found herself on edge as she quietly rose to her feet.

Eliza could see a figure coming towards her now, though because of the soft lighting, she could not quite make it out. It wasn't until they were just a few meters away that Eliza was finally able to decipher who was headed her way.

"Willis," she exclaimed. "What on earth are you doing in this wing at this time of night?"

"Oh, Lady Montagu, you gave me quite a fright! I wasn't expecting anyone to be out."

"Me either."

"Right. Of course. Sorry," he stammered.

"What are you up to, Willis?" Eliza asked again. His failure to answer her question the first time was making her increasingly suspicious.

"I—Mr. Barnsley gave me a letter. Said it was absolutely urgent that I post it immediately."

At the mention of Barnsley, Eliza's ears perked up. She'd been so distracted by the question of Molly's child's paternity that she had utterly forgotten about Barnsley, but at the beginning, he had been her prime suspect. Perhaps her first instinct had been correct.

"Give that to me, Willis. I'll take care of it for you."

"Oh, thank you, Miss, but that's not necessary."

"I know," Eliza said with a wink. "But give it to me anyway, won't you?"

Willis stared at Eliza for a moment. She could tell he was trying to calculate out in his head whether defying her would be worse than failing to follow through on his commitment to Barnsley. Much as she hated to use her position in the family, she knew she had to do something to stack the deck. Seeing the contents of that letter was far too important to let humility get in the way.

"I'd hate to have to tell Parkins that you refused a request from a lady of the house," she said pointedly.

And just like that, the letter was in her hands.

She didn't even wait until Willis was all the way gone to begin opening it. It was hard to read in the darkness of the hallway, but if she squinted a bit, there was just enough light for her to make out what it said.

As soon as she did, her stomach leapt into her throat. This was it. Her smoking gun.

She knew who the killer was. The real one this time.

CHAPTER TWENTY EIGHT

Eliza's initial instinct was to wake up the Inspector and tell him everything, but as she walked through Thistlewood on the way to his room, she began to realize that this may not have been an ideal plan.

After all, she was the one who identified Molly as the murderer. Coming to him with a different theory of the crime just a few hours later might make her seem like the girl who cried killer. She wasn't sure that she could convince him without proof, and the closest thing she had to proof was that letter. And the very last thing she wanted was to show him that.

She needed a different approach, some tactic that would allow her to reveal the salient information from the letter while also keeping her family's private business private—and that's how she decided on the breakfast.

Eliza knew the Darlingtons would be leaving in the morning, and, having been proven very wrong in a very public setting, Lady Darlington might not be exactly eager to socialize. She also knew, however, that absolutely no one in this house could resist a piece of juicy gossip. They lapped up each morsel the way Scout lapped up Rene's clotted cream. So, she decided to plant a seed.

After leaving Cedric's room, Eliza went back to see Rene. While she was there, she asked him to let it slip to one of the maids that she had made a big decision about her future, which she would be announcing to the family the next morning at breakfast. She knew the rest would take care of itself.

Sure enough, the rumor of Lady Eliza's big announcement spread like wildfire through the servant's quarters, and by the time the family and their guests had begun waking up, every lady's maid and valet was speculating about what this announcement could be. Was Lady Eliza going to follow her parents' wishes and be wed to Jacob Darlington? Was she going to strike out on her own and accept a life of poverty as a result? Or was she returning to Thistlewood for good, unwilling to marry the new Lord Darlington but also unwilling to embark on a pauper's journey?

No one had answers, it seemed, but everyone was quick to share their opinions, and just as Eliza hoped they would, the Ladies maids and valets were equally quick to raise this topic of conversation with the Lords and Ladies at Thistlewood that morning while helping them prepare for the day. The Darlingtons and Fairfaxes may have otherwise chosen to forgo the meal in favor of getting an early start on their journey home, but they weren't about to skip breakfast now—not when there was such delicious gossip to feed on.

Eliza couldn't help but smile when she entered the dining room for breakfast that morning. She loved it when a plan came together, and this had done so splendidly. As she surveyed the table, each person sitting exactly where she'd hoped they'd be, she felt like a master puppeteer. Even Inspector Abernathy was right where she needed him to be—not in the room, which Eliza thought might set people on edge and therefore make them less forthcoming, but in the room next door where he could hear everything without being seen. He had been lured there by Frank, to whom Eliza had promised a handsome tip for his troubles.

Eliza took a seat between Melville and Mercy. The servants entered with sterling silver trays piled high with delectable offerings—the Chelsea Buns she'd helped Rene make the night before, bacon, eggs, blood sausage, scones, jam, and clotted cream—but all eyes stayed glued to Eliza.

She was tempted to draw things out a bit, just to heighten the anticipation, but then she remembered Molly. Eliza thought about how scared she must feel, pregnant and alone in a prison cell, waiting to be tried for a murder she did not commit, and suddenly nothing felt more important than executing her plan as quickly as possible.

"I have an announcement to make," Eliza said. "As you know, I was integral in identifying Molly as the person who killed Lord Darlington, but it would appear I've made a mistake."

"Eliza—" Cedric said, the terror in his voice readily apparent.

"Do give me moment, brother. This is not about you," she said pointedly. She could tell from the look on his face that he had absolutely no idea where she was going with this, but her words were enough to at least bring some of the color back into his cheeks.

"It's not about Molly either. It's about Lord Darlington. Despite appearances, Lord Darlington was, it seems, an absolutely terrible businessman. Before his death, he ran the business into the ground. In fact, he was just days away from having to file for bankruptcy when he was killed."

"This is preposterous," Lady Darlington said, but Eliza just continued on without even so much as a moment's pause.

"I assure you it's not, Lady Darlington. I have seen the ledger. His man, Liam, buried it in the woods in hopes that it would die with Lord Darlington, but some secrets just cannot stay buried."

"If you knew about this ledger," Oliver interjected, "why didn't you say something sooner?"

"Because I didn't think it was relevant. The man was already dead, Ollie. I saw no reason to kick dirt on his grave."

"I don't believe you," Lady Darlington insisted. "You may not be a murderer, but you are a liar and a disgrace to your family's name."

"Think about it, Lady Darlington. You said yourself that a marriage to me was beneath Lord Darlington. You also said you were only here on his insistence. Why would he insist on coming here if business was good?"

Lady Darlington had no answer for that.

Eliza scanned the room quickly. She could tell people were starting to piece things together, but there were still portions of the puzzle that they could not quite solve.

"Lord Darlington was planning to scam us—to present himself as a wealthy businessman in hopes of securing my hand, therefore taking over our family business and using it to prop up his own. He almost got away with it too. He probably would have if he hadn't been found out by the one person who had the most to gain from his death."

With that, Eliza turned and stared at Jacob.

"Jacob, you knew, didn't you?"

There was a collective gasp at the table.

"I—"

"Don't bother answering. I have proof that you did," Eliza interrupted. "You knew your brother was destroying the family business. He was cruel and incompetent, and the fact that he still got everything filled you with rage. You knew you could do better, but as the second born, you would never have the opportunity. Not while he was alive, anyway."

"This is absurd," Jacob said, pushing back his chair and rising as though he was preparing to leave the table.

"You did everything you could to shield yourself from suspicion. You showed up here pretending to be the carefree younger brother who wanted nothing to do with the burdens of heirship. You even planted the poison in Molly's room when the investigation took too long to reveal an alternate suspect, and then you steered me to her by planting the story of your brother's inappropriate behavior with the help."

"There's a problem with your ludicrous theory. I never served my brother any food or drink. I never had an opportunity to slip anything in his food or glass. So how the devil do you suppose I poisoned him?" he said. He was haughty now, and there was nothing Eliza was looking forward to more than showing him he wasn't half as smart as he thought he was.

"I thought quite a bit about that, actually. You almost had me. I spent hours last night trying to figure out precisely how you'd done it, and for a while there, I wasn't sure I would ever find an answer. But then, it hit me. The poison wasn't drunk. It was inhaled."

Jacob was doing a remarkable job of keeping his composure, but there was a moment, just a flicker of recognition, when Eliza mentioned the method of poisoning. He knew he was in trouble. He knew she had him. And Eliza knew it too.

She turned to Liam then, who Willis had brought in just minutes before at Eliza's request.

"Liam, who would typically have packed Lord Darlington's pipe?" she asked.

"I would have, m'lady."

"But who packed it the night of the murder."

"The victim's brother, m'lady."

Suddenly, the room became electric. Everyone was buzzing with conversation, and the tension in the air was palpable.

"I will not stand by and listen to these absurd allegations one moment longer," Jacob said. "We're leaving, right mother?"

He turned to Lady Darlington, clearly expecting her to leave, but she just stared at him. It was unclear to Eliza whether she was currently experiencing heartbreak or rage, but the one thing she was sure of was that Lady Darlington wasn't going anywhere with Jacob. Not now and probably not ever.

Unwilling to wait any longer, Jacob began storming out of the room, but before he could leave, Inspector Abernathy appeared in the doorway.

Right on cue, Eliza thought.

"I think you and I need to have a chat," Inspector Abernathy said.

Jacob froze for a moment. Eliza could see him doing calculations in his head, trying to determine the next best move. And then suddenly, he shoved Inspector Abernathy out of the way, and started sprinting out the door.

Wrong choice, Eliza thought, as she pulled up the hem of her dress and started running after him.

CHAPTER TWENTY NINE

Jacob Darlington raced out of the dining room, down a narrow corridor, and into the grand hall—the Inspector, Eliza, Scout, Cedric, and Melville all fast on his heels. As he rounded the corner near the spiral staircase, he ploughed right into a servant. The servant fell backwards, and the trunk he was carrying sprung open, spilling all of its contents on the floor. Jacob, however, never even broke his stride.

He must have run track at Cambridge, Eliza thought, given the unbelievable speed and agility with which he was navigating every imaginable domestic hurdle.

Jacob had put at least ten meters between himself and everyone else by the time he flung open the French doors and began sprinting down the marble stairs. Eliza and the rest of the crew trailed along behind him, dashing out of the house and down into the garden.

The moment they stepped outside, Eliza knew Jacob's plan. She could see it in her mind's eye. Someone operating on instinct would have tried to head for the road—either by running there or trying to take one of the cars. The problem with both of those plans was that it left far too much time for one of his pursuers to catch up to him. Sure, he had put considerable distance between himself and everyone else, but it wasn't sustainable. If he took either of those routes, he would surely be caught.

The problem with Jacob Darlington was that he was smart. Worse, he was a planner. He thought strategically about everything, always carefully plotting out his next move and doing everything he could to stay three steps ahead, so Jacob wouldn't just operate on instinct. Eliza knew he would have spent every second of their run through the house planning his escape—working to identify ways to simultaneously shield himself and slow everyone else down. And with that train of thought, she knew there was only one place he could go: the hedge maze.

Eliza was right, of course. The moment he set foot on the grounds, Jacob began making a beeline for the hedge maze. He sprinted around the rose garden and the fountain, past the weeping willows and wisteria, and then into the hedge maze, all the while with the Inspector, Eliza, Scout, Cedric, and Melville in hot pursuit.

Eliza could see the look of defeat that passed over Inspector Abernathy's face as Jacob entered the maze. He could see the wisdom of Jacob's plan. There was just one mitigating factor neither Jacob nor the Inspector had correctly accounted for: Eliza.

Eliza had spent countless hours in the hedge maze as a child. She had explored every inch of it and memorized every twist and turn. When she was younger, she often used this knowledge to hide from her mother or Great Aunt Martha when they wanted her to do something Eliza found either repugnant or excruciatingly dull. It had been years now since she'd done that, but it didn't matter. That maze was forever burned into Eliza's memory.

She kicked off her shoes at the entrance to the maze so that she could run faster, and then she let muscle memory take over. A left, a right, and then another left followed by three rights. Running through this maze was just as Eliza remembered it. Perhaps better even.

Eliza never ran anymore. It was the sort of thing grown women—particularly ladies—just didn't do. Even as a young child, her mother had expressed concern anytime Eliza ran. It wasn't the sort of thing one expected from a Lady. It was not, as Mother said, an appropriate way to present themselves to the world. "True ladies," her mother would say, "never rush."

For all of the ways in which Eliza defied convention, for some reason, she had listened to her mother on this. Over the years, she had slowed down. She had ceased to run. She had never realized what a loss it was until now. There was something about that feeling—about her legs pumping as fast as they could while her cheeks flushed and her hair blew recklessly in the wind—that felt like freedom. And as she ran, she vowed she would never let society or family opinion take that from her again.

Twenty-seven turns later, Eliza arrived at the end of the maze. The fact that it had been so long since she'd last run had caught up with her, and she found herself doubled over, desperately trying to force air back into her spasming lungs. She did not, however, find Jacob.

I must have beaten him to it, she thought. There was certainly no way he'd gotten there before her. No one could have done that unless they'd memorized the maze, and Jacob simply had not had the access to the garden required to do so.

Eliza paused for a moment to plan her next move. She could stay here and wait for Jacob, knowing that he would either find his way out, in which case she could catch him, or get lost somewhere inside the maze, in which case he would likely be caught by one of the men. Objectively, that made waiting seem like the logical choice, but it nevertheless felt to Eliza like the wrong one. She didn't want to give a mind like Jacob's any more time to plan an escape than was absolutely necessary.

"Want to help me find him, boy?" Eliza said to Scout.

She certainly didn't have to ask the dog twice. He took back off into the maze before Eliza could even so much as blink.

Eliza ran back into the maze, looking down each row in search of Jacob, but there was no sight of him. Scout had run so far ahead that Eliza couldn't see him anymore, but she was reasonably confident that he would alert her if he saw anything. Luckily, she turned out to be right.

A few minutes after re-entering the maze, Scout started barking ferociously. Eliza knew that bark. She recognized it from the time they found Liam in the woods. Scout had Jacob. She was sure of it.

Because of Eliza's knowledge of the maze, it didn't take long for her to trace the sound of the barking and locate Scout. He was standing outside the entrance to the secret garden. Of course that's where Jacob had gone! He must have assumed no one knew about it other than Eliza, and it likely didn't occur to him that a woman would have successfully joined the hunt.

The danger of outdated thinking, Eliza thought with a smile as she pulled back the hedges, allowing Scout to sprint ahead of her through the rhododendron tunnel.

Eliza entered the hidden garden just in time to see Scout apprehending the suspect. Apparently, on hearing Scout coming, Jacob had tried to escape, but Scout was on him before he could—biting him on the ankle and sending him tumbling over backward, across the swing and onto the grass with an impressive thud.

Eliza rushed over to Jacob who was lying on the ground, the wind clearly knocked out of him.

"Hello, Jacob," she said as she put her foot on his chest in an effort to ensure he would not run away. "Fancy seeing you here."

Jacob couldn't seem to manage words just yet. Instead, he just stared up at Eliza, his face a palpable combination of misery and fury.

"Oh boys," she called out. "I've got him!"

"Where are you?" Cedric shouted.

"The secret garden," Eliza replied.

"What?" she could hear Melville ask.

"Just follow me," Cedric replied.

A moment later, Cedric, Melville, and Abernathy appeared. Eliza could not help but smile at their expressions as they took in the scene.

"Well done, Miss Montagu," the Inspector said as he walked over to Jacob. "I can take it from here."

Eliza took her foot off of Jacob and crossed back over to Scout.

"Good boy," she whispered as she scratched under his chin.

"Good boy indeed," Cedric replied.

"I'm not one for creatures," Melville said. "Too much work and all that. But this one—this one's alright."

Eliza grinned as she, Scout, Cedric, and Melville began the trek back to the main house. A crowd had gathered on the steps of Thistlewood House, and Eliza, Cedric, and Melville were immediately accosted for answers and information the moment they arrived. Before they could even so much as get out an answer, however, everyone's attention was drawn back into the grounds, where Inspector Abernathy appeared just a few feet behind them, hauling a handcuffed Jacob Darlington in tow.

The group followed Inspector Abernathy and Jacob back through the main house and out the main entrance. They watched, alternating between stunned silence and hushed whispers, as the Inspector pulled up his car and began loading Jacob into the backseat. As he did, Jacob made eye contact with Lady Darlington.

"I did it for us," he yelled to her. "Can't you see it? He was ruining everything. I had to do it. I had no other choice."

Lady Darlington said nothing. She only turned and walked inside as her son continued screaming "I did it for us!" to her back.

CHAPTER THIRTY

The Fairfaxes and Lady Darlington both left shortly after Jacob's arrest. Eliza had planned to leave right away too; she was eager to get back to her flat—back to her life—but Cedric asked her to stay. Molly was getting released that evening, and if he was going to have a chance of ever looking her in the eye again, he knew he needed to take responsibility for his actions.

The first step in that process would be telling the family what he'd done, and he knew that was not going to go over well. He had never defied their parents before, never even so much as mildly disappointed them, so this felt like foreign territory. He wanted moral support from someone who had tread these boards before, and, well, Eliza certainly fit that bill.

She sat next to him that night at dinner. She could practically feel his nerves vibrating through the table. He was terribly fidgety, constantly bouncing his knee or picking at his fingers, and he barely ate a bite of Rene's famous Beef Bourguignon. By the time dessert came— an absolutely stunning array of chocolate souffles—Eliza was worried that his heart might explode from the pressure.

"Just tell them," she whispered, grabbing Cedric's hand under the table and giving it a gentle squeeze.

"I can't."

"You can."

Cedric studied Eliza's face for a moment as though he was trying to absorb her confidence through the sheer power of staring. Eventually, he closed his eyes, inhaled deeply, and turned his attention to the rest of the table.

"I have an announcement to make," he said quietly.

"Oh dear," Great Aunt Martha said. "Two announcements in one day? I'm not sure I can handle this level of excitement."

"Will this one also end in a foot race?" Melville asked. "Because if so, I really should stretch this time. The last one was murder on my calves."

Mercy laughed, but Eliza stayed uncharacteristically quiet—a fact her mother immediately noticed.

152

"What's going on?" Lady Montagu asked. "Has something happened?"

"In a manner of speaking," Cedric began. "As you know, Molly is being released this evening."

"The maid?" Lord Montagu asked.

"Yes. The maid. And also…" Cedric paused for a moment to summon his courage. "…And also, the mother of my child."

Lady Montagu dropped her fork, and the silver made a sharp clink against the china. It echoed loudly through the dining room, which was otherwise eerily silent.

"And here you all thought it would be me that would bring shame to the family," Melville said, finally breaking the silence. He laughed at that, though no one laughed with him.

"Who else knows?" Great Aunt Martha asked.

"The chef," Cedric replied. "But no one else, to my knowledge."

"That's something, at least," Lord Montagu replied. "He was planning to leave anyway."

"Good," Lady Montagu said. "Good. We can keep it quiet then. We'll need money, of course. She won't leave without it. How much, do you think?"

"What?" Cedric asked, stunned by both the question and the calmness with which this was all being handled.

"How much money will it take to get her to leave and keep this quiet? Have you discussed it with her?"

"I—"

"No matter," Lady Montagu interrupted. "Whatever it is, we'll pay it. Though, of course, you shouldn't tell her that. It would hardly make for a strong negotiating position."

"I don't—" Cedric stammered, taking a breath and trying to focus himself before continuing. "I don't want to ask her to leave. I love her, and I want to raise this child with her."

For a moment, everything was silent again. It was almost as though the revelation was so shocking that the family had been frozen in time. And then, suddenly, everyone erupted. It was so loud and so chaotic that it was difficult to understand what anyone was saying. And then, suddenly, Lady Montagu stood up, her voice rising above the clamor.

"Enough!" she yelled.

Again, the room went silent. *Say what you will about Mother*, Eliza thought, *but she always did know how to command a crowd.*

"Cedric, you are the eldest in a prestigious family. And this family takes precedence. Always. So, you will not marry this girl and you will not raise this baby with her. You will pay whatever it takes to send her away and send this scandal off with her. And that is final. Do you understand?"

Lady Montagu didn't even wait for Cedric to respond. She simply said "good," and then stormed out of the room.

Cedric turned to Eliza. He said nothing, but she knew what he was asking anyway.

"I'll do my best," she whispered before standing up from the table and going in search of her mother.

She found her in the garden, furiously pruning a rose bush that was decidedly not in need of pruning.

"Not now, Eliza," Lady Montagu said before Eliza had even had a chance to open her mouth.

"Mother, I know you're disappointed, but—"

"I am not disappointed, Eliza. Disappointed is what you feel when dinner is late or your favorite dress doesn't fit. Not what you feel when the one child you thought was on the straight and narrow path threatens to torpedo the family name and legacy."

"I understand this is upsetting," Eliza began, "but sending her away is not the answer. Cedric loves her, and you don't want to put him in the position of choosing between the family who raised him and the family he's made. And you certainly don't want that child growing up without ever having a chance to know their father do you?"

Lady Montagu didn't say anything. She just kept furiously pruning.

"There's not going to be any bush left if you keep going like that," Eliza said, gently taking the shears from her mother's hand.

"Mother, you always told me that family was the most important thing. If that was true for us, that is true for this child too. They deserve a chance to know their family. And we deserve a chance to know them."

Lady Montagu still stayed silent, but Eliza could tell that her resolve was weakening. She was getting somewhere. She could feel it.

"How about this? Let Molly stay on the estate. Cedric doesn't have to marry her, and no one needs to know the child is his—not yet anyway. But this way, he can at least be part of their lives. We all can."

Eliza searched Lady Montagu's face for any hint that her argument had been successful. The longer she looked without answers, the further her heart sank. After everything Cedric had done for her growing up, she so wanted to do this for him. She knew he would make a wonderful father.

But then, suddenly, just when she had almost given up all hope, Lady Montagu nodded.

"Alright," she said. "I will allow it for now. But I reserve the right to change my mind."

"Of course, Mother," Eliza said with a smile. "I would expect nothing less. You should go tell him now. Cedric will be delighted, and the rose bush could use a break."

With that, Eliza headed back inside. She was eager to book her train ticket back to London, but first, there was one more thing she had to do.

Eliza found her father in his study. She knew he would be there. It was always the space he retreated to when things were difficult. The door was partly open, but she knocked anyway before poking her head inside.

"Come in, my girl!" her father said with delight.

She took a seat in an armchair by the fireplace, and as he'd done when she first arrived, Lord Montagu got up and poured his daughter a whiskey. She savored it and the space for a moment. She didn't know how long it would be before she was back here again.

"What can I do for you?" her father asked as he sat down in the chair next to her. "I take it from your expression this is not a social call."

"No, it's not, I'm afraid."

Eliza took another sip of her whiskey as she summoned her courage. Unlike with her mother, Eliza had always felt like she could tell her father anything. But this—this was hard to say.

"I know," she said finally.

"Know about what, darling?"

"I know why you brought in Barnsley here. I know he was supposed to be appraising things in the house—helping you streamline your assets in hopes of liquidating enough cash to keep the business afloat. I know things have been bad for a while now and Cedric's lack of business sense and Melvlille's lack of...well, sense, have made them infinitely worse. I also know that Barnsley wasn't who he claimed to be. He was in cahoots with Lord Darlington to try and steal from us."

"No, that's not—"

"It's true, father. I intercepted a letter from him to Darlington's lawyer. That's how I knew about Jacob."

Lord Montagu stared at Eliza for a moment. He was clearly in shock. And then, suddenly, he looked away. He was too ashamed to look his daughter in the eye, and that broke her heart.

"I have full faith in your ability to turn things around, Father," she said, attempting to summon a bit more confidence than she felt at the moment. "But there is no way you can continue to pay for my flat while you do so."

"Eliza—"

"No, Father. Don't argue. You know it's true. But it's alright. It's about time I make my own way anyway. And I will. You'll see."

"So, you're going back to London then?"

"Yes," she said with a smile, "and this time, I'm going to make it on my own."

***

Eliza stood outside of Thistlewood the next morning, squinting into the summer sun with her siblings as she waited for Stevenson to pull the carriage around and take her to the train station.

"I'm going to miss you," Mercy said, her eyes welling up with tears as she hugged Eliza.

"I'll be back," Eliza assured her. "And you must read some Kate Chopin while I'm away. That way, we can talk about it upon my return."

"We'll all miss you," Cedric said.

"Me especially," Melville added. "Who's going to take the heat off me while you're away?"

Eliza laughed.

"I think Cedric may have that handled for you," she said with a grin.

"I take it back. I won't miss you a bit. London can have you," Cedric replied with a wink.

"Your ride, ma'am," Stevenson said, once again popping up behind Eliza without her noticing.

"I think, on my return, we may have to put a bell on you Stevenson," she said with a grin.

"I'll look into it, Miss," he said, and though he never smiled, Eliza thought she detected the slightest hint of a twinkle in his eye.

"Eliza, my girl," her father's voice boomed from out the window to his study. "Travel safe. We'll miss you."

Her mother stood at the window too, but she said nothing. In fact, she hadn't said a word to Eliza since discovering that Eliza planned to return to London. That stung a bit, but Eliza was thankful she at least wasn't trying to stop her.

"I'll miss you too," she called up to her father before turning her attention back to her siblings. "I'll miss all of you."

With that, she followed Stevenson to the carriage. She was surprised to find that she had mixed feelings about her departure. While the idea of going back to the city felt absolutely right, there was also something about leaving Thistlewood behind that felt wrong. The truth was, Eliza realized, no matter where she lived, this place would always be her home.

As they pulled away, she turned back to catch one last look at Thistlewood House.

Until we meet again, she thought, as the horses carried her forward into her new life.

EPILOGUE

Eliza shivered as she stepped out onto the streets of London. An autumn chill had just begun to settle into the air, and she pulled her peacoat a little tighter as she started the thirty-minute trek to her flat from the National Gallery.

After Eliza returned to London, for the first time in her life, she found herself in need of a job. Much as she wished to make a living as a painter, she knew that was not an option—at least not yet—so she'd gone in search of the next best thing: a job that would at least allow her to be around art all day. One of her suffragette sisters had a connection to the National Gallery, and she got Eliza an interview for a position as a docent. Eliza's education and travels made her a perfect fit, and they hired her on the spot.

She'd been there for a month now, and she loved it. The pay wasn't much, but it was enough to pay for her small flat on the outskirts of town. Plus, she got to spend all day every day showing people around the museum, talking about their collections and highlighting some of her favorite pieces. She would have done that for free.

It was well past seven PM when she began the climb to her fourth-floor walkup. Her feet ached from standing all day, and she was absolutely starving, but she had no plans to stop for dinner or rest. She had a painting in her head, and she was desperate to get it onto canvas.

Eliza opened the door to her studio apartment and made a beeline to her easel. She took off her beret and coat, shook out her hair, and grabbed her paints. She had just started sketching when there was an unexpected knock at the door.

Oh, hell's bells, Eliza thought as she sat down her pencil. *Why did interruptions always have to come right when she was at her most inspired?*

She made her way to the door and peered through the peep hole. She did not recognize the man on the other side, but he appeared to be holding a letter.

"Can I help you?" Eliza asked as she unlocked and opened the door.

"I have a letter for you," the man said. "It's marked urgent."

Eliza stared at the letter for a moment. She could tell immediately from the seal that it was from someone at Thistlewood.

She thanked the man and closed the door before heading over to a small desk in the corner of her apartment. She pulled out her letter opener and pulled it gently across the top of the envelope.

Dear Eliza, it read in handwriting she immediately recognized as her father's. *Things with the business have gotten worse and, try as they might, Cedric and Melville are no help. Would you consider coming home? We need you. Oliver Fairfax is in town again, if that helps make the request any more attractive.*

Eliza stared at the letter for a moment, unsure what to do. She had a life in London that she loved—one that, for the very first time, she had built entirely herself. But Thistlewood was her home, and her father said her family needed her. He had never said anything like that to her before. Plus, there was the question of Oliver Fairfax. Whatever there was between them, she would never figure it out while she was here and he was there.

Eliza loved it here in London, and she had no desire to leave. But in her heart, she knew what she had to do. She had to return to Thistlewood—this time, maybe for good.

NOW AVAILABLE!

THISTLEWOOD MANOR: A DOLLOP OF DEATH
(An Eliza Montagu Cozy Mystery—Book 2)

"Very entertaining. I highly recommend this book to the permanent library of any reader that appreciates a very well written mystery, with some twists and an intelligent plot. You will not be disappointed. Excellent way to spend a cold weekend!"
--Books and Movie Reviews, Roberto Mattos (regarding *Murder in the Manor*)

THISTLEWOOD MANOR: A DOLLOP OF DEATH (AN ELIZA MONTAGU COZY MYSTERY—BOOK 2) is Book #2 in a charming 1920s cozy mystery series by Fiona Grace, #1 bestselling author of *Murder in the Manor*, which has over 300 five star reviews!

For centuries, Thistlewood Manor has stood as home to the Montagu family, a beacon to British aristocracy in rural England. But it's 1928, and in this new age of women's rights, Eliza Montagu, 27, a free spirit, has turned her back on her family to live an artist's life in London.

Yet after Eliza is summoned home, she decides to stay (for now) to help her father run the ailing family business. The presence of her childhood best friend, Oliver, also gives her a reason to stay, as she wonders if their unfulfilled romance might ever come to fruition.

Fall has arrived, bringing to town major Fall festivals and celebrations in the gorgeous countryside—and yet also bringing to town a female suitor who wastes no time trying to woo Oliver away. Seeing Eliza as her rival, the suitor does everything she can to malign her and make her life miserable.

And when a servant turns up dead, poisoned by a slice of pie meant for Eliza, all eyes fall on the suitor. Did she mean to murder Eliza?

Was the pie meant for someone else in the family? Or for the suitor herself?

Eliza, realizing she is implicated, is forced to solve the perplexing murder—and ends up utterly stunned at what she discovers.

A charming historical cozy mystery series that transports readers back in time, THISTLEWOOD MANOR is mystery at its finest: spellbinding, atmospheric and impossible to put down. A page-turner packed with shocking twists, turns and a mystery that's hard to solve, it will leave you reading late into the night, all while you fall in love with its unforgettable heroine.

Book #3 in the series (CALAMITY AT THE BALL) is now also available.

Fiona Grace

Fiona Grace is author of the LACEY DOYLE COZY MYSTERY series, comprising nine books; of the TUSCAN VINEYARD COZY MYSTERY series, comprising seven books; of the DUBIOUS WITCH COZY MYSTERY series, comprising three books; of the BEACHFRONT BAKERY COZY MYSTERY series, comprising six books; of the CATS AND DOGS COZY MYSTERY series, comprising nine books; and of the ELIZA MONTAGU COZY MYSTERY series, comprising three books (and counting).

Fiona would love to hear from you, so please visit www.fionagraceauthor.com to receive free ebooks, hear the latest news, and stay in touch.

BOOKS BY FIONA GRACE

ELIZA MONTAGU COZY MYSTERY
MURDER AT THE HEDGEROW (Book #1)
A DALLOP OF DEATH (Book #2)
CALAMITY AT THE BALL (Book #3)

LACEY DOYLE COZY MYSTERY
MURDER IN THE MANOR (Book#1)
DEATH AND A DOG (Book #2)
CRIME IN THE CAFE (Book #3)
VEXED ON A VISIT (Book #4)
KILLED WITH A KISS (Book #5)
PERISHED BY A PAINTING (Book #6)
SILENCED BY A SPELL (Book #7)
FRAMED BY A FORGERY (Book #8)
CATASTROPHE IN A CLOISTER (Book #9)

TUSCAN VINEYARD COZY MYSTERY
AGED FOR MURDER (Book #1)
AGED FOR DEATH (Book #2)
AGED FOR MAYHEM (Book #3)
AGED FOR SEDUCTION (Book #4)
AGED FOR VENGEANCE (Book #5)
AGED FOR ACRIMONY (Book #6)
AGED FOR MALICE (Book #7)

DUBIOUS WITCH COZY MYSTERY
SKEPTIC IN SALEM: AN EPISODE OF MURDER (Book #1)
SKEPTIC IN SALEM: AN EPISODE OF CRIME (Book #2)
SKEPTIC IN SALEM: AN EPISODE OF DEATH (Book #3)

BEACHFRONT BAKERY COZY MYSTERY
BEACHFRONT BAKERY: A KILLER CUPCAKE (Book #1)
BEACHFRONT BAKERY: A MURDEROUS MACARON (Book #2)
BEACHFRONT BAKERY: A PERILOUS CAKE POP (Book #3)
BEACHFRONT BAKERY: A DEADLY DANISH (Book #4)
BEACHFRONT BAKERY: A TREACHEROUS TART (Book #5)
BEACHFRONT BAKERY: A CALAMITOUS COOKIE (Book #6)